THE *UNLISTED*

BOOK ONE

JUSTINE FLYNN   CHRIS KUNZ

SCHOLASTIC

Published in the UK by Scholastic Children's Books, 20XX
Euston House, 24 Eversholt Street, London, NW1 1DB, UK
A division of Scholastic Limited.

London – New York – Toronto – Sydney – Auckland
Mexico City – New Delhi – Hong Kong

The right of Chris Kunz and Justine Flynn to be identified as the author of
this work has been asserted by the Author under the Copyright, Designs
and Patents Act 1988.

ISBN 978 0702 30104 9

A CIP catalogue record for this book is available from the British Library.

Printed by CPI Group (UK) Ltd, Croydon, CR0 4YY
Papers used by Scholastic Children's Books are made
from wood grown in sustainable forests.

1 3 5 7 9 10 8 6 4 2

www.scholastic.co.uk

Dedicated to the young people who are brave enough to question the status quo – the future belongs to you

PROLOGUE

The abandoned alleyway in the dark, dirty forgotten part of Sydney wasn't quite pitch black – but it was close. It was only six-thirty and night was beginning to fall, but the only thing moving here was one of the resident rats out in search of food scraps. It stopped suddenly and sniffed the air, just a nanosecond before a black van veered too quickly around the corner and slammed into the brick wall of the manufacturing plant. The excruciating sound of metal slamming into brick echoed down the alleyway as the van's headlights flickered for a moment and then died. An eerie silence followed. The rat scurried down a nearby gutter amid the hiss and creak of the crumpled van.

Then came a loud scraping sound as the van door was slowly wrenched open from the inside, and a teenager fumbled her way out, battered and bruised. She wore an oversized white jumpsuit and a fearful expression. She scanned the alleyway before nodding to someone back in the van. Two more teenage girls and a boy climbed out, wearing matching jumpsuits. Despite the crash, they all seemed okay. Suddenly they all turned and ran down the alleyway, as if their lives depended on it.

Inside the van, the driver, dressed in a black special forces style uniform, struggled to open the door. His colleague in the front passenger seat leaned over to help and they both pushed until the door opened and they climbed out, stumbling and groaning. Despite soreness and probably whiplash, they knew they had a job to do. One of the men pointed down the alleyway. 'Hey! Stop!' he shouted, his gruff voice the only sound interrupting the sinister silence. When it was clear the kids were not going to follow instructions, the two men started to run after them.

Up ahead one of the girls tripped and fell, sending her round wire-framed glasses flying off her face. The boy rushed back. 'Gemma, get up. Quick!' he hissed as he helped her to her feet. He passed Gemma her glasses. 'Thanks Jacob.' They looked back and saw the men running towards them, so they quickly took off after the others.

They reached a street corner, and disappeared out of sight of the angry men chasing them.

•

It seemed like only seconds later, but in reality three minutes had gone by, and the game of cat and mouse continued. The four teens were still running. The two men were still chasing. Gemma and Jacob, along with Kymara and Rose, were fatigued but no less scared. In the distance they could see the Opera House. Rose wondered for a moment how anyone could be out enjoying themselves while they were running for their lives. They ran down a steep set of stairs near Sydney Harbour. The natural leader of the group, Rose, spotted a CCTV camera mounted on a light post. Realising they would stand out wearing their white prison jumpsuits she immediately hid her face and signalled for the others to do the same.

At the bottom of the stairs, she dodged between moving cars to bolt across the road, and the others followed. Rose glanced back up to the top of the stairs and saw the guards still giving chase. The group ran on but heard a screech of tyres behind them and drivers shouting abuse at the guards as they continued their pursuit.

The four ran down a street, past kerbside restaurants, raising the eyebrows of a few diners wondering if the group was wearing costumes for some sort of fancy-dress party. Jacob, passing an Italian restaurant with an outside table yet to be cleared, smelled something he couldn't resist. He stopped to grab an abandoned garlic bread.

Rose, a little way ahead, saw him do it and rushed

back to him as he took a furtive bite. 'What are you doing? Come on!' She grabbed him by the arm and they caught up with the other two, slipping down a side street.

The teens' pursuers hit the bottom of the concrete stairs and ran straight out onto the road to try to get a clear sight of which direction the kids had gone. One of the men was nearly taken out by a passing car. The horn blared, the car swerved to avoid impact – but they continued their hunt, oblivious to the insults hurled by the angry driver.

The four teenagers raced down another flight of steps, and slammed to a halt in front of a huge metal archway. It appeared to be the entrance to some sort of underground tunnel system and was the only direction they could go, but the tunnel was blocked by an imposing double gate locked by a heavy chain and a massive DO NOT ENTER sign. The teens looked at one another for an instant, making a joint decision: *We have no choice.* The chain holding the gate together was wide enough to pull apart a little so the kids could slip through. Jacob held the chain so Rose could climb through first, and then Kymara and then Gemma before he followed, hurrying behind the others into the darkness.

Just as they disappeared out of sight, the men, still in pursuit, ran past the top of the stairs. One stopped and glanced down at the gate, shrouded in darkness and locked by the heavy chain, before deciding to move on, running further into the night.

•

The four teens ran through a train tunnel, trying not to fall in the shadowy light. The ground was rough, uneven, littered with stones and rubbish, and they had to keep looking down to avoid tripping over the rusted train tracks. Kymara spied a nook in the wall, a recess where all four could rest for a moment, catch their breath. They all shuffled in and stood close together, crammed into the small space, their chests heaving and their voices hoarse.

As Jacob started to lean backwards to see out into

the tunnel they were all struck by a sudden ear-splitting squeal as a freight train barrelled down the line. Jacob threw himself against the others and, along with Rose and Kymara, blocked his ears and shut his eyes. Gemma, terrified and exhausted, screamed, her eyes wide open, but the sound of her fear was drowned out by the roar of the train's engine.

CHAPTER ONE

Drupad Sharma's hands are tied to the dentist's chair. He is sweating heavily, his eyes wide, listening to the sound of a drill he cannot see getting closer and closer to him. He tries to scream for help, but no sound comes from his choked-up throat. He struggles against the ties restricting movement to his hands, but they are so tight the cords cut into his wrists. The more he fights, the greater the pain.

He can't remember why they tied him down. Perhaps he'd tried to run. It wouldn't surprise him; he has lived his whole life terrified of dentists. He hates the loud, sharp noises. He hates the coldness of the instruments. He hates the large hands of the dentist. Even the angle of the dentist's chair makes him shiver. But did they really need to tie him so firmly?

The dentist approaches. Dru can't see their face, hidden behind a surgical mask, but even if he could he probably wouldn't notice any details — all he can see is the sharp metal drill that has appeared in his vision. The shrillness of the drill's whine gives him an instant headache.

The dentist pulls open Dru's mouth, causing him to shake in panic. There is no way he can handle the pain that is only a couple of seconds away . . .

He glances past the shady silhouette of the dentist and gasps.

His twin brother Kalpen is there, smiling, holding his finger to his lips, silently telling Dru not to let the dentist know he's there. But if he doesn't intervene soon, it's going to be too late. Dru's eyes widen as he looks at his twin. Hurry, Kal, hurry! *as the drill tunnels into Dru's mouth —*

•

'Argh!' screamed Dru from the safety of his warm bed. The thirteen-year-old woke up, dripping with sweat, and panting hard. He rubbed his eyes, tried to slow his breathing back to normal, and reached over to his bedside table for his glasses.

From the other side of the bedroom, his twin groaned. 'Keep it down, would you.'

Dru knew where he was now. Everything was going to be okay. It was just his dentist nightmare again. None of it was real, none of it apart from his brother being nearby. He looked over at Kal, still shaken. 'I had that dentist nightmare again.'

Kal yawned, completely uninterested. He rolled over to try to get a little more shut-eye when a loud *bang* on their bedroom door made Dru leap into the air, still wired from his nightmare.

The twins' grandmother, their *dadi*, pushed open the door. She wore a golden *salwar kameez*, like a beautiful long dress shirt, with matching cotton pants. Dadi greeted them with a loud, 'Rise and shine, my little wombats!' Seeing the boys still looking sleepy, she let off a party popper. The boys knew their dadi was quite dramatic, but this was extreme, even for her.

As colourful streamers shot into the air, Dadi announced, 'Up, up, up! It's Diwali!'

So *that* was the reason for the party popper. Diwali was Dadi's favourite day of the year. It was the Hindu festival of lights, and one of the most celebrated festivals for Indians around the world.

Both boys grinned at their grandmother. 'Happy Diwali, Dadi.'

Like a colourful whirlwind, Dadi disappeared to wake up the next unsuspecting Sharma with a loud knock.

Kal smirked at his brother. 'Even Dadi scares you?! How are we even related?'

'Ugh. Too early,' they heard from their sister's room as sixteen-year-old Vidya got the same treatment from Dadi. The party popper popped and Vidya screamed. The boys giggled. Their sister was so not a morning person.

•

Breakfast at the Sharma house was always an event and the kitchen was the heart of their home. Dadi loved cooking for her son Rahul and his family. His wife Anousha, daughter Vidya and twin sons Dru and Kal loved Dadi's cooking, so it was win-win. Today Dadi had prepared traditional Indian flatbread *parathas* for the family and they were seated around the dining table, happily awaiting another delicious breakfast. Rahul and Anousha smiled at their three children; everyone knew how special this day was for their dadi.

The Sharma home was a bright, light-filled two-storey house in the leafy suburbs of Sydney. Inside, the house was filled with wooden and brass Indian artefacts – elephants, water pots used as vases, vibrant wall hangings. Photos of the family lined the hallway and took up every spare inch of space, each boasting a flower garland as a sign of respect.

Dadi handed out parathas to the family as she explained what needed to be done today. 'Kal and

Dru – cleaning duties after school. I want to see my reflection in everything.'

'You look beautiful this morning, Dadi,' Kal enthused. 'But I think it's Dru's turn to clean this year.'

Dadi smiled at her grandson. 'Nice try. The two of you will work together.'

Dru shot an angry look at his twin.

'Come on,' Dadi warned in a voice filled with laughter but also a little bit of steel. 'No fighting on Diwali, wombats. It breaks your dadi's heart.'

Rahul and Anousha chuckled at their boys' grumpy expressions. They all knew it wasn't worth arguing with Dadi on Diwali – or any day, really. She was the matriarch of the family. She had moved to Australia from India when her first granddaughter, Vidya, was born, and had been an important part of the family ever since. When Anousha gave birth to twins three years later, Dadi was already running the household like a professional. It meant that Anousha could return to her beloved work at a research lab, and Rahul could continue his work as a baker. None of the Sharma children remembered life without their dadi. She was the one home in the mornings to get them ready for school, and the one who was there in the afternoon, supervising homework, and ensuring they were properly fed. She was invaluable. And, it seemed, invincible.

Dadi handed out parathas to her son and daughter-in-law, as Rahul turned up the volume of the radio he always had close by: *World leaders gather in Shanghai to debate the long-term effects of climate cha—*

The silence was sudden as Dadi grabbed the radio from Rahul and turned it off.

'Mum! I was listening to that,' said Rahul.

'Too bad. The leaders are all corrupt anyway . . . they're hiding the cure for cancer, you know,' responded Dadi.

Dru hid a smile. He knew this wouldn't go down well with his science-obsessed mother.

'No, they're not, Dadi,' huffed Anousha. 'What have we said about filling the kids' heads with conspiracy theories?'

Dadi ignored the reproach, and put a paratha on Vidya's plate. 'Today you're in charge of decorations, my little emu.'

'It's officially my Diwali wish to change that nickname,' her granddaughter replied.

'Ah well, good luck to you,' said Dadi with a grin.

Vidya was willing to give it an extra push. 'Won't Ganesh be angry if you don't listen?'

Dadi ruffled her granddaughter's hair. 'Ganesh has bigger things to worry about, little emu.'

Dru finished his breakfast with a contented sigh. But then he remembered his dream. He turned to Kal and said quietly, 'You were in the dream this time.' An idea suddenly came to him; he didn't know if it was a memory from his dream or his mind playing tricks. 'I think Aunty Maya was the dentist.'

'Dreams should be more interesting than that,' Kal said firmly. 'Really. Stop going on about it.'

But the bad feeling the dream had given Dru stayed with him as he cleared the breakfast dishes with his twin. When he got back to his bedroom the dread was almost overwhelming and even though he'd had dreams like this before, he decided it was worth risking trouble from his parents by taking a quick look at an online dream dictionary before school, to see if he could work out what it might mean. His computer ban for hacking had been in place for one month and he didn't like deceiving his mum and dad, but just one quick look . . .

'To dream of the dentist means an untrustworthy presence is about to enter your life. You must take care not to —'

His reading was interrupted by a knock at the door. Dru shut his laptop and quickly slid it under his bedcovers. 'Come in.'

His mum and dad entered with big smiles, and sat either side of Dru on his bed. 'Since it's Diwali, we've decided to lift your computer ban,' said Anousha.

Dru swallowed guiltily but worked to cover it as Kal entered their room.

Rahul added, 'But you need to promise us, no more hacking.'

'As if,' snorted Kal.

His mother ignored Kal, and kept her focus on Dru. 'We mean it. We don't want another call from your school,' she said.

Anousha and Rahul tried to hide their smiles. 'We know you're clever, *beta*,' said his mum.

'But we want you to use your powers for good,' finished up Rahul.

Dru tried to look sincere. 'I will. I promise.' He saw Kal glance over to his bed, and then not-so-subtly spot the outline of the laptop hidden underneath the covers. Kal shook his head, obviously disappointed their parents were so gullible.

'Right, well, I've got to get back to the bakery and it's time for you kids to get to school,' said Rahul as he and Anousha left the room. 'Have a great day, boys.'

'Can't believe you got away with that, bro,' said Kal, running his fingers through his hair, untucking his shirt and admiring his appearance in the wardrobe mirror.

Dru glanced over at his twin. Dru knew that although they were identical twins Kal always managed to look cooler than he did. They went to the same barber but Kal's black hair sat better and even though they were both tall and lean, his brother was just that little bit more athletic and coordinated. They had access to the same wardrobe but somehow Kal's clothes always looked better. It was annoying, but Dru had always got higher marks at school, and he was quieter so, although he wasn't popular with the other students, the teachers generally liked him. That was something, he reminded himself as he straightened the glasses on his nose.

On their way out the front door, Dru and Kal stopped by Dadi, who handed them their lunch tiffins. 'Don't forget your Diwali duties,' she called out after them as the twins fastened their bike helmets. 'And don't be late!'

CHAPTER **TWO**

Dru was pedalling fiercely to stay slightly in front of Kal – until Kal noticed and put in a bit of extra effort to overtake him, leading the way through the suburban Sydney streets to arrive at the school grounds a moment before his twin.

As the boys parked their bikes just inside the gates of Westbrook High School, Kal said, 'You might be smart, but you lose every time.'

Dru ignored Kal's usual jibe about his lack of sporting prowess, instead looking around him, suddenly wondering if the dream dictionary might have any basis in reality. Should he be on the lookout for an 'untrustworthy presence'? He let his gaze wander around the schoolyard. Everyone seemed the same. Same teachers, same kids, same grey uniform.

Dru and Kal had never really hung out together and didn't sit near each other in class. Although they got on just fine, it had become clear when they were both in primary school that they had different personalities and different interests. Their parents had never dressed them the same, much to Vidya's disappointment, and the friends they'd grown up with never really thought of them as twins. Anyway, Dru wearing glasses made it easy to tell them apart.

Kal was staring at him, waiting for his response to the jibe.

'It wasn't a race,' said Dru.

Kal nodded with an exaggerated smile. 'You keep telling yourself that.'

'Dru! Kal!' Chloe Flannery waved and jogged over to them. 'Happy Diwali.' Chloe, with fair skin and long red hair, had been the boys' next door neighbour their whole life and Dadi made sure Chloe was included in all their special family celebrations.

Dru wasn't great with girls, and even though he had known Chloe forever, he still struggled to keep it together *around* her. He thought she was really pretty, which made it a hundred times worse. He tried to act natural. 'You remembered,' he said, coughing self-consciously.

Kal rolled his eyes, embarrassed by his brother's embarrassment.

Chloe, on the other hand, never seemed to notice Dru's nervousness around her. 'I've been counting down. Can't wait for Dadi's party tonight.'

'You're coming?!' Dru knew he sounded too eager, and tried to backtrack. 'I mean – come if you want.'

Chloe smiled. 'Okay then,' she said quietly, 'see you later.' Dru grimaced. He tried so hard to play it cool around Chloe.

Kal looked at Dru with amusement. 'Smooth.'

The bell rang over the school's PA system, followed by an announcement: 'Good morning, students and staff. It's Mr Park. My year group will be participating in the Global Child Initiative dental plan today. Please head directly to the sick bay instead of homeroom. Thank you.'

The blood drained from Dru's face. 'Oh no,' he said. 'No, no, *no.*'

•

At the sick-bay door, Dru was next in line, sweaty, shaking and terrified. Chloe, who was well aware of Dru's squeamishness with dentists – she remembered Dru sobbing when he lost his first tooth – was right next to him in the line. She did her best to calm him down. 'Think of it this way: at least we get to miss history.' Dru's expression told her the optimism wasn't working.

The door to the sick bay opened and Kal stepped out, as cool as a cucumber.

'How was it?' Chloe asked.

Kal scoffed. 'Easy as.'

Chloe turned to Dru. 'You're next.'

Dru gestured to the door. 'Ladies first,' he said shakily.

Chloe smiled. 'Thanks Dru.'

Once she'd gone in, Dru turned desperately to Kal. 'I can't do this. Can you go in for me?'

Kal, annoyed by his brother's request, said, 'Nope. I've already done you a favour today.'

'What?'

'I didn't tell Mum and Dad that you were on your computer the whole time you were banned.'

Dru couldn't deny that, but he still couldn't bear the idea of facing the dentist. 'Please. It's Diwali.'

Kal raised an eyebrow. 'Yeah, nah.'

The twins' bargaining was interrupted by a sudden shout from down the corridor. Kal's best friend, Tim Hale, marched out of the sick bay away from Miss Biggs, the school's Wellness Officer. 'My parents didn't give permission!'

Kal called out to Tim. 'Hey Tim, you okay?'

Miss Biggs stepped out of the sick bay, calling after Tim. 'I'm sorry, young man, but the check-up is compulsory.'

Tim bolted down the corridor, disappearing from

view, leaving a furious-looking Miss Biggs to turn to Mr Park, their class teacher, with a grimace, before heading back into the sick bay.

Mr Park was the favourite teacher of nearly all the students. He was always reliably laid-back and genuinely seemed to care.

Mr Park took the unspoken cue and headed up the corridor. 'Tim! Tim, come back!'

Dru realised this was the perfect opportunity to do the hard sell on his brother. 'Quick! Now! No-one's watching. I'll give you my pocket money for a month.'

Kal knew an opportunity when he heard one. 'Deal.'

Dru quickly passed his glasses to Kal, who put them on as the door opened and Chloe stepped out. She turned to Kal and put her hand on his shoulder. 'Don't worry, Dru, it only hurts for a second. You'll be fine.'

Dru tried not to look like he was squinting without his glasses. He was incredibly relieved as his brother entered the sick bay a second time.

•

In the sick bay Kal once again sat in the dentist's chair, with his head back. Now out of his brother's sight, he was feeling a little worried that the dentist would realise he'd already been in for a check-up.

Miss Biggs, a lean, hollow-looking woman whose smile always looked more like a grimace, hovered nearby as the dentist, Dr Goodman, stepped towards him. 'Okay, Dru. We're going to do a check-up and gum treatment. You'll just feel a little pinch and you may experience some residual pain for the next day or two.'

This is exactly what had been said the first time.

Dr Goodman opened Kal's mouth and put the dental drill in, focusing on the left side, as she'd done last time. Kal pulled back, making a noise. The dentist removed the drill.

'Can you do the other side?' he asked.

'May I ask why?'

Kal came out with the first thing he could think of. 'I have an ulcer. Too much Indian food.'

Dr Goodman looked to Miss Biggs. 'I don't see why not . . . now, close your eyes.'

Kal closed his eyes and opened his mouth as the sound of grinding started up.

A moment later, it was all over. Kal opened his eyes to see the dentist removing her gloves and washing her hands. Miss Biggs was tapping away at a tablet, entering data.

Miss Biggs looked over to Kal. 'You're free to go, Dru. Please send in the next student.'

•

'You owe me big time,' said Kal as he handed back Dru's glasses on their way to their classroom. Before he had the chance to continue the guilt trip, Regan Holcroft shoved past them to get to her favourite seat.

'Hey!' said Kal, annoyed.

'Out of my way, Sharmas!'

Regan was a tall girl with perfectly straight, light brown hair and a bad attitude. She competed with Kal in sport and against Dru in all things academic. Dru could ignore her but she infuriated Kal. Regan and Kal were both hyper-competitive and natural leaders and just rubbed each other up the wrong way. Always had.

Kal moved to the back of the class, glaring at Regan while Dru sat up the front.

'All right everyone,' Mr Park said as he handed out papers to the class. 'We have a surprise test courtesy of the Global Child Initiative.'

The students moaned.

Kal's hand shot up. 'Sir, I feel sick.'

Regan was not impressed. She rolled her eyes and said, 'Don't fall for it, Mr Park. He's totally fine.'

Mr Park continued to hand out the tests, ignoring the fuss.

Dru was perplexed. 'But, sir, we haven't studied.'

'I'm sure you'll be fine, Mr Sharma. Relax.'

Dru wasn't satisfied with Mr Park's glib response, and shot his hand up in the air in the hope of getting the teacher's attention. But before he could speak the class door swung open. Miss Biggs entered the classroom, carrying an iPad and looking carefully at the students before announcing, 'Excuse me, Mr Park.

For a moment Dru thought he was having another nightmare. His first instinct was to cry out, yet something deep in his stomach kept him quiet. He slumped down a little in his seat and tried to look around without attracting Miss Biggs' attention. She stood watching the class from the back of the room, seemingly unperturbed by the radical change in the students' behaviour. Her attention switched between the students and the tablet in her hand, not noticing that Dru was not affected like the others were.

Dru was trying not to hyperventilate. He quickly adjusted his body – he didn't know what was happening but he knew he didn't want Miss Biggs to see him move. He could hear other students talking and walking past the door to the classroom, so whatever had happened had only affected the students in this class. And he was pretty sure Miss Biggs had expected it to happen; that she had come to the classroom and got rid of Mr Park in order to watch it happen. Miss Biggs stood directly in front of the class, holding the tablet and inputing information.

In his peripheral vision Dru could see she was pleased with what she saw. Just when Dru started to think he should try to sprint out of the classroom to get help, the students broke out of their stasis. Dru sat back upright and watched as his classmates went back to working on their tests, as though nothing had happened.

Regan caught Dru looking at her, and poked her tongue out at him. Dru looked down at his test, trying to stop his hands shaking. Miss Biggs urged the class to finish their tests, though she continued to watch them closely.

Although the rest of the period went by without anything out of the ordinary, Dru couldn't concentrate. He kept expecting everyone to zone out again. He knew the answers he handed in at the end of class were well below his normal standard.

As the kids filed out of class after the test, Dru waited for Kal and pulled him aside. 'What happened in there? You froze for, like, minutes. Everyone froze. Everyone but me!'

Kal scoffed. 'That's 'cause the test was hard. And you're a nerd.'

'It's the strangest thing I've ever –'

Dru bumped into the student in front of him before realising everyone had stopped dead in their tracks. Kal too. They remained standing but it was like they'd been zapped by something. Miss Biggs, sitting at the teacher's desk, looked over at the kids, her face showing concern. Dru stood completely still, mimicking his brother and classmates without even knowing why, only that he felt it was the safest thing to do.

Miss Biggs pulled out her mobile phone and dialled a number. 'I'm with the class at Westbrook High. I think we have a glitch.' She listened for a moment and then responded. 'You can try rebooting it, the new update might have overloaded the system. Turn it on and off.'

A moment later the students returned to life and continued moving out the door as the school day ended. Dru kept up with them, unsure what was going to happen next but too scared to say anything.

Kal continued the conversation from earlier, as though nothing had happened. 'Don't know what you're talking about, bro.'

Dru was still in shock as they made their way to their bikes. He felt scared and unsure of what to do. They climbed on their bikes and started to ride home. Dru stared at his brother. 'Are you sure you're feeling all right, Kal?'

Kal responded, 'Never better,' before accelerating so fast that he disappeared out of sight of his twin in seconds.

Dru stared after his brother, shaking his head. *What the heck was going on?*

CHAPTER **THREE**

By the time Dru made it home, Kal was already in the kitchen drinking a glass of juice. Dru stared at him, wondering if he was going to freeze again, but he was just being his annoying regular self.

Dadi and Vidya were also there, preparing the food for Diwali. Vidya, her long black hair tied back into a ponytail, already looked like she was resenting having to be Dadi's helper. Vidya was not keen on cooking and would have much rather preferred to be in her room. She was trying to open a jar of ghee but it was stuck.

'You have to put your back into it!' Dadi encouraged her granddaughter.

'It's not budging,' said Vidya, frustrated.

Dadi turned to the twins. 'We've tried everything: a wet towel, tapping it seven times with good intent –'

Kal finished his juice. 'I'll do it.' He grabbed hold of the jar, gave the lid a quick, easy twist and the jar shattered.

Dadi and Vidya screamed in unison as glass exploded everywhere.

'Whoa!' Kal stared at his hands in shock.

'How did you do that?!' demanded Dru.

They all stared at Kal, stunned.

Dadi was shaken. 'Are you hurt?' she said, moving to Kal's side. She examined his hands. 'Did the glass cut you?'

Kal looked down at the glass, surprised by the mess he'd made. He tried to comfort his grandmother, 'Nope, I'm fine.'

Dadi looked at the broken jar. The ghee had oozed out onto the floor, which was littered with glass shards.

Now she knew her grandson had not been injured, her attention moved to her party planning. She gasped in horror. 'It's ruined! No ghee means no food, no lamps. You can't have Diwali without light!' Every year the Sharma family had a Diwali party. The house was decorated with lights, Dadi cooked all their favourite food and everyone dressed in their best traditional clothing.

Kal knew how important today was to his dadi. 'It's okay, Dadi. I'll get you some more,' he offered.

A glimmer of hope sparkled in his dadi's eyes. 'Good boy. You'll have to be quick.' She reached for her purse on the bench and passed him some money. 'You go while I tidy this up.'

Dru followed Kal outside to the driveway. 'Something's going on for sure. You just broke a glass jar with your bare hands!'

'Stop with the conspiracies, Dru. You're worse than Dadi.' Kal grabbed his bike and put on his helmet.

From inside the house Dadi called out, 'Dru! We have a million things to do!'

'Can't Dad help?' Dru called back.

Dadi appeared at the front door. 'He's still at the bakery.'

'And Mum?'

'She's doing Pilates in those tight pants. Why? Don't you want to help your dadi?'

Dru knew he'd run out of options.

Kal smirked at his twin's defeated expression, and immediately Dadi frowned at Kal. 'And *you*. What are you still doing here? Ghee!'

Kal jumped on his bike and rode off just as Chloe arrived at the Sharma's front gate. Dadi had always treated Chloe like part of the family. Even when she was a toddler Chloe would come over for play dates. She loved the smell of the food and spices in the Sharma kitchen and the matriarch of the house adored the little ginger-headed girl who was always interested in trying Dadi's meals. Chloe had soon become a permanent fixture at all important gatherings.

'My child!' Dadi threw up her hands in welcome. 'Come, come! I need all the help I can get.'

Chloe grinned at Dru as Dadi ushered them all back inside the house.

Dru blushed. The only thing he wanted to do was run up to his bedroom and google 'freak extreme strength' and 'alien mind control', but his inclination was thwarted by Dadi's mania to have everything spotless for tonight's party. Without Kal to help, Dru was tasked with double the work – dusting, vacuuming, polishing and fluffing cushions.

Next on Dadi's never-ending list of jobs for Dru was to help Chloe with the *rangoli*. 'Come on, kids,' Dadi enthused, 'we must do everything we can to invite Lakshmi to visit us.'

Dru had grown up admiring the intricate coloured patterns his dadi insisted they create on special festival days, all in the name of the goddess Lakshmi, but it was tricky work done by hand. Chloe and Dadi set to work with the vibrantly coloured powder, Chloe putting in maximum effort. Chloe always volunteered to make the rangoli, she loved focusing on the patterns and making sure the lines didn't smudge. Dru half-heartedly helped, which was better than Vidya's contribution. She was 'busy' painting her nails.

'Couldn't we have just bought pre-made rangoli?' Vidya asked.

'Sure, why not? Just grab it off the eBay!' Dadi answered sarcastically, causing Dru and Chloe to stifle a laugh.

Vidya swung her foot out to admire her new nail polish and accidentally knocked over a pot of red powder. 'Oh, I'm *so* sorry!' She frowned at her toes. 'I'm going to have to do another coat.'

Dadi glared at the spilled powder. 'This is not a good omen,' she mumbled, gesturing for Dru to help her clean up the mess. 'The ghee I could ignore. But now this.'

Dru brought over a newspaper and dust pan and brush. He started to sweep up the red powder while Dadi went in search of a cup of calming chai.

The headline on the newspaper caught Dru's eye.

GLOBAL CHILD INITIATIVE HELPING STUDENTS REACH

PEAK PERFORMANCE. There was an accompanying photo of a group of medical staff with logos on their coats.

Curious, Dru pocketed the page and looked up to see Chloe watching him.

Dru's words stalled before he could speak them aloud. Had Chloe seen what he'd seen at school today? Had anyone? He was too nervous to ask, in case Chloe thought he was losing the plot. 'So . . . what's new?' he blurted awkwardly, instantly cursing himself for not asking the question he really wanted to ask.

'Kymara Russell posted a really weird video,' Chloe said suddenly, breathlessly. 'It's the first she's posted in a while. And now it's disappeared.'

Vidya was instantly interested. 'Do you follow Kymara Russell?'

Dru answered before Chloe could. 'Everyone follows her. She's *the* gaming guru.'

Chloe was concerned. 'Something weird's happening, Dru. I think she's in real trouble. She's been offline for a bit.' She leaned in close to her friend, talking quietly. 'She posted a really strange video and then – nothing. She seemed scared, not her usual self. It was really freaky, you've got to see it. Can you find a video that was taken down?'

'I promised Mum and Dad no hacking,' replied Dru.

Chloe looked at Dru with her big puppy-dog eyes. 'Please?'

As if Dru could possibly resist. 'Okay, but we'll have to be quick.'

Vidya rolled her eyes as the two raced upstairs to the twins' bedroom. 'Slackers.'

•

Dru and Chloe were huddled at Dru's desk in the twins' bedroom. Dru was in full geek mode, explaining as his fingers danced over the laptop's keys. 'See here? I have to hack into her account to find deleted content.'

Chloe nodded, encouraging.

'I really shouldn't be doing this.' He paused, and Chloe sighed. Even a hint of disappointment from Chloe was enough to get Dru typing again. He was a natural when it came to finding his way into a computer network. Occasionally his parents used his talents to help out with an issue they were having with their work computers or to help sort out the home's wi-fi but they were not supportive of his interest in hacking. It had landed him in all sorts of trouble. 'Okay, look. A video was removed two hours ago.'

'That's it!' said Chloe.

Dru pressed play. On the screen was a close-up of Kymara's face as she ran – it had been a live stream on her phone. Kymara, her face full screen, her eyes wide with fear, her voice trembling. 'Hey, Kymaniacs! No game news today. I won't be able to post for a while, but, there's something I have to tell you –' And then the frame went black as a hand covered the lens.

A girl's voice yelled, 'Stop it! Give me that!'

With the screen still black, Kymara could be heard yelling, 'Don't trust anyone! Things are not what they seem!' Then the image shuddered – the phone had been dropped – and the last image was the sole of a boot about to stomp on the screen.

Chloe looked concerned. 'Weird, right? I think she's in trouble.'

Dadi's voice echoed from downstairs. 'Dru? Chloe? The rangoli won't finish itself!'

Chloe stood up to return to Dadi but Dru was focused on something else. He went back a few frames until Kymara was again on screen. He zoomed in to what she was wearing. It looked like a white shirt although he couldn't see much of it. But what he could see caused him to frown. 'That logo.'

Chloe paused and looked at him uncertainly. 'Dru? Are you coming?'

He nodded vaguely and she left the bedroom. Dru pulled the newspaper article from his pocket and compared the logos. They were identical. An orange cube that was framed by another cube. But before he could crosscheck anything else his mobile phone buzzed. It was Kal.

'Have you got the ghee?' Dru asked his brother.

'I've tried three Indian grocers and there's none left,' replied Kal, sounding stressed. 'Everyone runs out the day of Diwali. I've found a shopkeeper who's got an emergency jar set aside, but he won't hand it over unless I can ask for it in Hindi.'

'Fine. Don't panic. I'll tell you what to say.'

His brother cut him off. 'No, it's on Addison Street. Just come over now. It'll be quicker if you ask. Your Hindi is much better than mine.'

Dru couldn't argue with that. He'd always loved the lessons Dadi had given the twins since they were little, and he was a fluent Hindi speaker. 'Okay, I'm on my way.'

•

A few minutes later Dru rode up to Kal. He was leaning against a wall, holding his bike outside the store. He looked annoyed. 'Do you know how hard it was to escape Dadi? Luckily Chloe was there to distract her.'

'Just buy the ghee, Dru. Consider it payback for the dentist.' Kal handed over the cash Dadi had given him.

Dru sighed at the mention of the dentist. The weight

of unanswered questions was increasing every moment.

'What are you waiting for, bro?' asked Kal impatiently.

'All right. All right,' said Dru as he entered the store.

Kal remained outside watching their bikes. Dru appeared in the entrance of the store a couple of minutes later, grinning. 'He said my Hindi is perfect.' Dru enjoyed provoking his brother.

'Yeah, yeah. Let's go.'

The brothers were about to head off when they heard a shout from across the road.

'Kal! Kal!' It was Tim Hale, looking dishevelled and scared. He was sweating hard.

'Tim! Are you okay?!' called out Kal. The boys hadn't seen Tim since he'd run away from the dental check that morning.

Tim stayed on the other side of the road. 'You can't trust anyone. Especially the Global Child people.'

Dru's ears pricked up. 'What do you mean?' he asked.

Tim responded, looking panicky. 'This dentist thing. They want to control us.'

Kal wasn't sure what to make of Tim. He was

normally so laid-back. Kal didn't know how to handle the situation. He looked intensely at his best friend. 'You're not making any sense, dude.'

Tim was getting more and more worked up. He kept looking over his shoulder. 'Don't tell anyone, or they'll be in danger too.'

At that moment a black van, driving fast, appeared from around the corner. Tim saw it and bolted like he was running for his life.

Kal called out after him, but Tim was already gone. Kal and Dru stood frozen as the van, which had tinted windows, slowed as it passed Kal and Dru. Then it suddenly performed a dangerous U-turn in the middle of the street and sped off in the direction Tim had run in.

That spurred Kal and Dru back into action. They didn't need to discuss what was going to happen next. They jumped on their bikes, following the van and Tim.

Kal was still unusually fast, and Dru struggled to keep up with him. Kal pointed to an intersection up ahead. 'There he is!' The van careened up the street as Tim disappeared down a smaller side road.

Dru raced to catch up with Kal. They screeched to a stop at the corner, unable to see where Tim had gone. 'Where did they go? Who's in the van?!'

Kal looked uncharacteristically scared. 'I don't know. We should tell someone.'

Dru shook his head. 'You heard what Tim said.' They both looked up the street, but the van was no longer in sight. 'And he probably got away. Right?'

Kal sighed. 'I really hope so. Come on. Let's go home.'

The twins rode off, this time side by side. They almost jumped out of their skins every time a van or bus drove past.

CHAPTER FOUR

When Kal and Dru arrived home, the floor was decorated with beautiful circular rangoli, one the size of a large pizza, the other twice as big again. They were filled with lovely colours of celebration – orange, pink, purple and outlined in white.

Dadi appeared from the living room, her good mood restored. 'I have never been so happy to see ghee! Vidya, the lanterns have been strung up outside. Go and light them. But be careful. They get very hot.'

Vidya went to leave but then turned back to Dru.

'Your girlfriend left . . . guess you'll have to save your flirt-a-thon for dinner tonight.'

The front door opened and Anousha stepped in, wearing activewear and looking a little messy post-workout.

Dadi frowned at her daughter-in-law's attire. 'Anousha, get changed! And shower. Goddess Lakshmi does not appreciate your sweat.'

Anousha laughed. 'Yes, Dadi!'

Rahul stepped in after her, carrying a tray of colourful Indian sweets, a lovely plate of bite-size special treats, little cakes and delicious sweet slices. 'Hi, Mum.' He handed her the plate.

Dadi gave him a big kiss on the cheek. 'Thank you, my beta. Now go. Get ready!'

•

In their bedroom, Kal was finishing up putting on his special Diwali *sherwani*, a long-sleeve smock style dress shirt, with loose-fitting pants and ornate slipper-like shoes. Dru was already wearing one, his a lovely matt gold silk, with gold cotton pants. Kal's was maroon in colour. Dru was sitting at his desk, trying to contact Tim via WhatsApp. Kal peered over his shoulder.

'Uh, a little space?' said Dru.

'Oh come on, you're the pro,' Kal chided.

'Tim's still not answering,' said Dru, frustrated. 'Try his phone again.'

Kal pressed redial on his mobile but there was no answer.

Indian prayer music began to blare from stereo speakers downstairs. 'It's game time,' said Kal. 'We better go.'

But Dru wasn't ready to give up yet. 'You go. I'll try one more time.'

Kal hurried downstairs as Dru tried WhatsApp again. 'Come on, come on.' He pushed recall for one last try and suddenly Tim's mum appeared on the screen.

'Hello, hello. Dru? Do you know where Tim is?' asked Tim's mum, looking very worried, her eyes swollen from crying.

'No, we're looking for him too,' replied Dru.

Tim's dad's face turned up on screen. 'He never came home from school. We're really worried.' His face looked more worn and aged than Dru had ever seen it before.

Tim's mum continued. 'And we can't get any answers out of the school.' Dru could see someone creep up behind the Hale's. 'Look out!' he cried. Mr and Mrs Hale both looked over their shoulders and saw two men in their kitchen. A moment later they were dragged out of sight. The line dropped out.

Dru was horrified, staring at the blank screen, unable to think about what to do next as he felt his heartbeat thump fast and loud. He had no idea what was happening. He had never felt this level of fear before.

The sounds of Dadi's Indian music eventually brought him back to the present. He reluctantly closed his laptop and was at his bedroom door when he heard Dadi ask, 'Where's –'

'Toilet,' Kal quickly answered.

Dru sprinted downstairs to take up his position in the annual Sharma line-up for Dadi's pre-Diwali inspection. The whole family lined up, dressed in their traditional costumes. Dadi, Anousha and Vidya wore beautiful saris. Dadi in an elegant maroon sari, adorned with lovely gold jewellery, Anousha in an elegant emerald and Vidya in a blushing pink. They looked beautiful. Rahul stood tall in his butter coloured sherwani, alongside Kal. Dadi placed a blessing hand on her son's head. 'Handsome as always.'

Dru tried to tamp down the fear that was still pulsing through him after watching the home invasion at the Hale house. What had happened to Tim's parents? Had they been kidnapped? Had Tim?

Dadi nodded, satisfied, and blessed both her grandsons just as the doorbell rang. 'Must be your *bua*,' she said to the children. Smoothing her sari, Dadi raced to the door.

'My darling daughter. The talented doctor,' said Dadi with love, greeting Maya with kisses and hugs. She continued in a boastful voice loud enough for the whole family to hear. 'Works such long hours helping people. Too busy to find a husband.'

Maya scoffed.

Rahul laughed. 'Stop giving her a hard time, Mum.'

As brother and sister gave each other a warm hug, Dru whispered to Kal, 'Tim's parents – I think they were kidnapped.'

Kal stared at Dru, confusion clear on his face, but he couldn't ask Dru to repeat his words because there were more family greetings to attend to.

'Hi family! Happy Diwali,' Maya said, giving Anousha and each of the children a hug.

'Hello Bua,' the boys said in turn.

'Save the hugging for later,' said Dadi, impatient. 'It's time to pray.'

The family followed Dadi to the lounge.

Maya walked beside Kal and Dru. 'Hey, you two. How's teenage life treating you?'

Dru shot her an unhappy look.

'Don't look so miserable, Dru,' she said with a laugh. 'You'll never be this carefree again.'

The twins looked at one another, horrified by the thought. Slowing their pace so the rest of the Sharma family moved ahead, the twins continued their hushed conversation. 'What do you mean Tim's parents were *kidnapped*?' asked Kal.

As Dru recounted what he had seen, Kal's eyebrows shot sky high. He was about to reply when Dadi gestured at them to join the rest of the family in front of the shrine to Lord Ganesh and Goddess Lakshmi. She picked up a platter of fruit.

Once the twins were seated, Kal turned to his brother. 'Are you sure?'

Dadi glared at her grandson. '*Sh.*'

The Sharmas passed a large silver tray between them. On it was a brightly glowing *diya*, a candle made out of the ghee that Dru and Kal had brought home earlier in the day. As the prayer music played, each family member waved the flame in front of the statues of the deities.

Kal whispered to his brother. 'Why would someone take them?'

'I don't know,' answered Dru.

Dadi moved between each family member with a small bowl that held Ganges River water mixed with milk. She stirred the water with her fingers to reveal gold coins. 'See the wealth. See the wealth, my children.'

Rahul and Anousha looked inside the bowl while the twins continued their whispered conversation. 'Tim said that this is all connected to the dentist,' said Dru. 'What happened in there?'

'I don't really remember,' answered Kal, and even though it sounded unbelievable Dru knew that his brother was telling the truth. Dadi stood, beaming at her family. Everyone had been blessed, night was falling and Diwali was about to begin.

Dru looked concerned as the doorbell rang again.

Dadi got up and headed for the door, saying, 'Okay family. Pretty faces on. It's time to party.'

•

Under the watchful eye of Dadi, the Sharmas certainly

knew how to throw a terrific Diwali party. The main festivities took place outside, where the backyard had been decorated with lanterns. There was lively conversation, many friends and neighbours, sparklers and enough delicious food to feed a small island nation.

Chloe stood talking with the twins. She wore a pretty gold sari that Dadi had given her, which used to belong to Vidya. Dadi was still in the kitchen, plating up the last of the sweets, small cakes and sugar coated almonds that Rahul had brought home that afternoon. Vidya sat with her mother and aunty at the table chatting and enjoying some of the nibbles. Rahul fussed about the garden, making sure the lanterns were all lit. Dadi came out of the kitchen and noticed a drooping chain of lanterns. She quickly zeroed in on her son. 'Rahul, *beta*, these lanterns are too low. Can you fix them, please?'

'On it,' said Rahul, and stood on a chair to reach the lanterns.

Dadi left him untying one of the cords and moved over to Kal, Dru and Chloe. 'Look at you three – so beautiful. Here – eat, Chloe. You too, my little wombats.' She handed the sweets tray to Kal just at the moment Rahul's chair tilted, causing him to slide off. The cord slipped from his hand, and a hot copper lantern swung loose, headed straight for Dadi.

'Look out!' called Rahul in a panic.

Kal jumped up and caught the burning hot copper lantern with his bare hand.

Dru watched his brother with a mixture of shock, fascination and concern.

'Oh Ganesh,' wailed Dadi. 'Are you burnt? Show me your hands!' she demanded.

Rahul rushed over. 'I'm so sorry. It slipped out of my grasp. Is everyone okay?' he asked.

'Everything's fine. I used the tray to stop it, not my hand,' said Kal, with a sidelong glance at Dru.

After everyone had admired Kal's hand-eye coordination and heroic actions, Dadi signalled at everyone to sit down. It was time to enjoy the feast she had spent the day cooking. Chloe moved to the table but the boys hung back. Dru grilled Kal. 'I saw what happened. There was no tray. How did you do that?'

Kal was still shaken. 'I don't know . . . but I swear it didn't even hurt.' He looked down at his hand. 'It should have at least burnt me.'

Dru's mind was buzzing as he tried to make sense of everything he had seen in the past twelve hours. 'It has to be the dentist visit, Kal. Since then, you've zoned out in class, broken a glass jar, rode your bike super-fast –'

'I *am* pretty fit,' Kal reminded his twin with the return of his confident grin.

'Yeah, but that doesn't explain how you caught a burning hot lantern with your hand!'

Kal couldn't argue with that logic. 'Maybe it's time to tell Mum and Dad what's going on?'

That was exactly what Dru wanted to do, but . . . 'We'd be putting them at risk,' he said reluctantly. 'Tim's parents started asking questions – and look what happened to them.'

Among the sounds of their friends and family laughing and enjoying Diwali, the festival of light,

Kal voiced what they were both thinking. 'So, we're on our own.'

•

At the same time in the same city, in a tunnel filled ankle-deep with water, the four teenage runaways were still moving, albeit much more slowly. Still wearing their white jumpsuits, which were now filthy, the four moved, heads down, through the murky water.

'Who even knew this place existed?' said Jacob, talking to keep himself from falling asleep on his feet.

Kymara stumbled. 'I am literally about to faint.'

Rose saw the exhaustion on Kymara's face. 'Come on. We need to find somewhere to rest.'

Gemma paused. 'I'm scared.'

Rose reached out a reassuring hand. 'Don't worry, Gemma. They'll never find us here.' Doubt crossed her face a moment later. 'At least, I hope not.'

CHAPTER FIVE

'Are you sure this is a good idea?' Dru asked his brother early the next morning.

'Come on. We still have an hour before we have to be at school,' Kal threw back at him as they approached the front door of the Hale house. 'Let's just have a look around.' He was about to knock when he realised the front door wasn't shut properly. It swung open with a creak. The twins exchanged a look. Kal pushed the door open and called out. 'Hello? Tim! Mr Hale? Mrs Hale?'

There was no reply from inside the house. Dru

made a quick sweep of the street to make sure no-one was watching, and then they stepped inside the house. He hung around the entrance hall. 'I don't feel good about this.'

Kal went further in, calling out, 'Hello, anybody home?' as he went. He was used to visiting Tim's house but usually his friend was home. Tim's house was like something from a Country Road catalogue, everything matched and was surround by cream coloured walls.

'Dru?' he called moments later. 'You better come look at this.'

Dru walked into the kitchen, trying to take hold of his nerves. 'Tim? Mr and Mrs Hale?' He stopped when he saw the mess. 'Whoa. This is bad.'

On the kitchen bench were takeaway food containers, plates ready for food, as if Mr and Mrs Hale had been interrupted before they had a chance to eat. The fridge door was open, and there was some food scattered around: noodles, spring rolls, and a plastic bottle was lying on the floor, water everywhere.

Kal looked around to see a vase shattered and flowers strewn, a mirror smashed, and a curtain hanging, half-pulled from the rail.

'Looks like they were dragged out of here,' Kal said. 'I'll check upstairs.' Kal disappeared for less than a minute and then reappeared to look at Dru, who stood frozen, purposefully not touching anything.

'There's no sign of them. We should call the police,' said Kal.

Dru shook his head. 'Tim said we can't trust anyone. We don't know who's responsible for this.'

Kal sighed, and Dru could see cracks in his usual bravado. Clearly he was worried for his friend. 'Let's get out of here.' Kal moved quickly back to the front door. Dru followed, happy to not spend a moment longer in this deserted, creepy house.

•

In the city at first light, the group emerged looking exhausted. Rose, Gemma and Jacob crept out of the shadows of an alleyway, heading towards a clothing donations bin. The teens were nervous, constantly checking around them to see if anyone was paying them any attention as they fossicked through the bags and boxes that had been dumped around the giant bin.

Rose reached into the overflowing bin and pulled out an old floral dress. 'Yuck . . . but we don't get to be picky.'

She grabbed an old backpack and started stuffing it with clothes.

Jacob searched through the boxes and pulled out a torch. 'Check this out.' He flashed it on and off. 'It actually works.'

Gemma found a pair of old walkie-talkies. She pressed the button on one and suddenly a crackle punctured the silence. 'These work too,' she said with a grin. 'Hey, we should –'

'Sh!' Rose said suddenly, and everyone froze. Seconds later they all heard footsteps and scrambled to hide: Gemma and Kymara threw themselves under the boxes and over-sized bags, while Rose grabbed

Jacob and shoved him awkwardly inside a bin.

A woman in running shorts and a singlet appeared around the corner, breathing heavily. She paused to check the fitness tracker on her wrist, frowned at it a moment, and looked over at the charity bin, the lid swinging ever so lightly. She walked towards it with a curious expression before her fitness tracker buzzed, telling her to keep moving. 'All right, all right,' she grumbled at it before starting to run once more.

Inside the bin, Jacob breathed a sigh of relief. Now all he had to do was work out how to get back out. He opened up the flap a little way. 'Rose!' he hissed. 'Gemma! Help?'

•

On the ride to school Dru kept an eye on his brother, looking out for any signs that yesterday's unusual behaviour would continue today. But Kal seemed fine, although judging by how fast he went on the bike, he had not lost his new-found strength.

The twins walked into school together, earning quizzical looks from a group of kids playing soccer. One called out, 'Oi, Kal! Where are you going? You're our striker.'

Kal glanced over, he rubbed his jaw, distracted with pain. 'Yeah. Later.'

Chloe bounced up to them a moment later. 'Hey, Sharmas? I really enjoyed the party last night. What are you up to?' she asked, full of her usual energy.

'What?' Dru said quickly, his paranoia kicking in. 'Nothing. What do you mean?'

Chloe grabbed him by the arm, mock-horrified. 'You missed chess club this morning.'

Dru stared at her in disbelief. But she was right: he had completely forgotten. He loved chess club and hadn't missed a session all year. He was about to try to come up with an excuse when a teacher's voice sounded over the PA system. 'Good morning students. Can Mr Park's year group please gather on the school field? This morning you will participate in the Global Child Initiative spot fitness text.'

'A spot fitness test?' repeated Dru, feeling nervous. What if the students freaked out like they did in class the day before?

Cheers and groans could be heard around the school grounds. For some it was time out of class, which was a bonus. For others it was sport, which was never something to celebrate. For Kal and Dru, if the Global Child Initiative was involved, it was sure to mean something far more sinister. Chloe wasn't sure why the boys stood still. She smiled at them encouragingly and gestured towards the field. They reluctantly followed.

As the students headed over to the sports field, the seriousness of this assessment became clear. It was only their year group, all the other students had headed to class. Miss Biggs was already overseeing the set-up of the test. Dru saw soccer ball cannons, a makeshift athletics field and a shot-put area, none of which eased his building nerves. Usually their PE teacher, Ms Capelli, would organise a class like this but she was nowhere to be seen.

The kids were soon lined up and assessments began straightaway. Dru and Kal waited in a long line to participate in shot-put. Miss Biggs held a stopwatch, and recorded times as the class cycled through sprinting, shot-put and goalkeeping. It was clear that many of the kids were feeling much stronger and fitter than they had done previously.

Dru watched, amazed, as one of his classmates ran a sprint. When Miss Biggs pressed stop on the stopwatch, Dru looked over at the number. His eyes grew wide. He whispered to his twin, 'Toby just ran a hundred metres in twelve seconds!'

Kal looked incredulous. 'What? That's impossible. The world record's like, ten seconds.'

They both looked over to another classmate as she lobbed a shot-put an impressive distance.

'And since when has Mandy Strazinski been able to throw like that?' asked Kal.

There was a lot of back slapping and spontaneous applause as the kids did far better than what they'd thought themselves capable of. But Dru also noticed a few of the kids rubbing their jaws, complaining about soreness. He turned to his brother. 'You all right?' he asked.

Kal was now also rubbing his jaw. 'I'm never covering for you at the dentist again. My jaw's killing me.'

'Tim mentioned the dentist. Did they do something in there to give you all, like, super strength?' asked Dru quietly as he and Kal made it to the front of the queue.

'Okay, Sharma twins, you're up.'

Dru didn't feel stronger or faster, nor did he have any jaw pain. He realised it wouldn't take long for Miss Biggs to suspect something was wrong.

Kal stepped up and hurled the shot-put a long way across the oval. He pumped his fist in the air and received applause from a couple of the students watching.

Then Dru had a turn and barely managed to throw the shot-put a couple of metres. Embarrassing.

Regan laughed. 'Loser.'

'Okay, Sharmas, your turn to move on to sprints,' said Miss Biggs, making notes on her tablet.

As the twins moved to the start of the sprint area, Dru leaned in to his brother. 'Whatever it is that's making you strong, I don't have it . . . I can't fail these tests or they'll know. You have to cover for me.'

Instead of answering, Kal hit Dru hard in the stomach.

Dru doubled over, clutching his stomach and groaning.

'Miss! Miss!' Kal called over Miss Biggs. 'My brother's sick.'

Miss Biggs hurried over, and Dru looked up, not having to pretend he was in pain. 'I think I'm going to vomit.'

'Are you all right?' asked Miss Biggs.

Regan stood nearby scoffing at Dru's discomfort.

'No, not really,' said Dru.

Miss Biggs appraised him with little concern. 'Straight to the sick bay, I think . . . just as soon as you've completed the fitness test. Now, come on, do your best.' She walked briskly away.

Dru straightened, annoyed with his brother for not giving him a warning and still gasping for breath.

As suspected, Dru performed badly on every test, while Kal excelled, stronger and faster than anyone else. After everyone had completed the assessment, the group was ushered back to class.

Miss Biggs came over to Dru. 'How are you feeling? Can you please come with me to the sick bay?'

'Um, I'm feeling a lot better,' said Dru, hoping to avoid any more intrusive assessments.

'Best to be sure,' replied Miss Biggs.

Dru caught his brother's eye and Kal nodded his understanding. He turned to Chloe, who was walking next to him.

'Hey, Chloe, I need you to faint.'

'What?' said Chloe, unsure she'd heard right.

'Just . . . faint. I bet you can't do it good enough to make anyone believe you. I'll pay you ten bucks.'

Chloe was always up for a challenge with a cash

reward. She collapsed dramatically in the corridor. The kids around her yelled for help, and Miss Biggs ran over.

Meanwhile Kal quickly moved to Dru's side. 'Give me your glasses. Hurry!'

Dru handed his glasses over and mussed up his hair, while Kal flattened his and adjusted the glasses and smoothed down his sport shirt. 'Here we go again.'

Chloe was slowly 'regaining consciousness', really hamming it up. Kneeling by her, Miss Biggs sat up straighter. 'Okay, Chloe – great performance,' she said, barely hiding the sarcasm in her voice. 'Time to get up now.'

Chloe looked hurt that the school's Wellness Officer clearly did not take her wellbeing particularly seriously, but she'd just earned a quick ten dollars, so all in all it had worked out well.

Miss Biggs glanced back. 'Where's Dru?'

'Right here, Miss,' said Kal.

She looked at both twins, confusion showing briefly on her face, before telling the one with the glasses to follow her to sick bay and the other to head back to class. 'Yes, Miss,' they said in unison.

Regan, nearby, looked at the twins suspiciously. She knew they hardly ever behaved like twins – so, what was going on with them now?

CHAPTER SIX

Miss Biggs guided Kal into the sick bay. 'Take a seat, Dru,' she said as she opened Dru's profile on her tablet. Her long bony fingers moved quickly across the tablet.

'I'm feeling a lot better now,' said Kal nervously.

Miss Biggs frowned at him, her steely blue eyes trained on his. 'Yes, you already said that.'

Kal tried to look blasé and decided it was best to keep quiet.

Miss Biggs took his blood pressure, heart rate, temperature and checked his pupil dilation, noting everything on her tablet. 'And open your mouth, please?'

'Why?' asked Kal.

Her thin lips tightened. 'So I can check your throat. For infection. You are feeling ill, aren't you?'

Kal nodded reluctantly. Miss Biggs picked up a couple of unusual implements and asked him to open wide, and took a quick look around his mouth.

'This seems fine. Healthy throat. Are you experiencing any pain in your jaw?' she asked.

'A little,' said Kal, although the truth was 'a lot'.

'That's to be expected. Now I'd like to just do a follow-up strength test.' Miss Biggs pointed to some gym equipment in the corner. Kal was surprised that the sick bay was now filled with fitness equipment. When he'd had a gastro virus a month ago, none of the equipment was there. It was probably part of the Global Child Initiative support the school had recently received.

'See if you can lift that kettle bell.'

Kal obliged, lifting the ten-kilogram kettle bell like it was a marshmallow.

Miss Biggs nodded. 'Can you go heavier? Try that one.'

Kal lifted a fifty-kilogram kettle bell over his head. Miss Biggs' eyes bulged with surprise. 'Well, you're a very strong boy, Dru. Just like your brother.'

Kal lowered the kettle bell.

'Do you ever get mistaken for one another?' asked Miss Biggs.

'Oh, no, I've got glasses, so –' Kal suddenly stumbled, feeling dizzy.

Miss Biggs reached out to stabilise him. 'Don't worry. This can happen when you push yourself too hard. Take it easy.'

Kal headed to the sick bay door, eager to get away. Maybe it just happened because he was wearing his brother's glasses and they made everything blurry. He picked up his bag. 'Okay. Thanks, Miss Biggs.'

Miss Biggs watched him go, unsmiling.

•

The twins had to pretend to be each other until after their geography class ended, when Kal found a moment to surreptitiously hand over Dru's glasses.

Poor Dru had squinted through the lesson trying to read what Mr Park had written up on the board about the difference between a water table and an aquifer, and hoping he didn't get asked any questions.

Near the end of lunch, Dru grabbed Kal from the soccer field and took him into the classroom. 'Why are we here?' asked Kal, annoyed. 'We're spending too much time together. I'd rather be playing soccer.'

Dru just rolled his eyes and started up the computer on the teacher's desk. 'Keep a lookout for me.'

Kal moved to the door, and half-heartedly glanced down the corridor. 'Can't you do this at home?'

'I need a networked computer. We have to find out how involved the school is in whatever's going on,' said Dru. 'Oh, this is interesting . . .'

'What?' asked Kal.

'They've tightened security.'

'Does that mean I can go back to my soccer game?' asked Kal hopefully.

'Huh? I'm in.' Dru looked smug. 'Genius. Whoa, check it! It's that logo again.' Kal moved from the door to take a look at the screen. He inspected the logo, which was made up of an orange cube framed by another cube above the heading INFINITY GROUP. In the bottom corner of the screen there was a folder that also had the words Infinity Group.

'Infinity Group. What's that?' Dru asked.

'Open it,' said Kal.

Dru double-clicked on the folder, and started to scan through the documents. 'Every kid in our year is listed here, and kids from other schools too! Looks like they're tracking us – biometric stats, locations, everything.'

'Nah, that's not possible,' scoffed Kal. 'How could they know all of that?'

Dru didn't answer but started to dig deeper. He opened a new window, and found a list of each of the students in the twins' class. Next to each of the names was one word: IMPLANTED.

Dru typed faster, opening up his file, with Kal's

next to it. He crosschecked the info on both. 'Our files are exactly the same – like, *exactly* the same. They have dates, locations, loads of data.'

Kal's eyes flicked back to the door. The hallway was still clear. 'Look up Tim's file.'

Dru nodded, found Tim's log, and read out, 'Hale, Timothy. Subject uncompliant. Implant rescheduled.'

Dru turned to his brother. But before the twins had a chance to say anything more, a warning message flashed across the computer Dru was using: 'UNAUTHORISED ACCESS!' An alarm blared from the speakers.

'That's not good,' panicked Dru.

'Shut it down. Shut it down!' hissed Kal, running back to the classroom door to see if anyone was coming.

'I'm trying!' answered Dru. But the system had frozen. He was trying to force quit but nothing was happening.

'Mr Park's coming! Hurry up!'

'It's not responding!' shouted Dru, sweat forming on his brow.

Kal opted for a less technical solution and dived for the wall, yanking out the power cord. The alarm stopped a half-second before Mr Park, who was listening to music and distracted, entered the classroom. A group of students followed him in. Dru and Kal merged as quickly as they could with the students, and took their normal seats.

'Okay, settle down, class. Now, dare I ask, how'd our algebra homework go? Any problems?' asked Mr Park.

The class remained quiet.

'Did anyone not do it?' he asked.

A few guilty hands went up, including Kal's.

Mr Park sighed. 'Honestly, guys. I want it by Friday. I'm not even joking.'

Miss Biggs knocked on the classroom door and entered, crossing directly to the computer on Mr Park's desk. She picked up the yanked-out plug and turned to Mr Park. 'Sorry to interrupt but the principal wanted me to let you know that there has been a security breach on this computer.'

Mr Park looked surprised. 'We've only just come

in from lunch.' He looked around the class. 'All right, who was it?'

The class remained silent.

Miss Biggs glared at the students. 'Global Child Initiative policy states that no student is to use a school computer without a teacher present.'

'And more importantly, you should never be on *my* computer,' added Mr Park.

Miss Biggs waited a moment, staring at each and every student. Dru felt beads of sweat gather across his forehead. Realising no-one was going to come forward, Miss Biggs sighed. 'Thank you, Mr Park,' she said with a strained smile. 'And further to that point, we need to work together to ensure a safe and happy school environment. If you see anything out of order, please report it to me.'

The Wellness Officer turned her attention to Regan. 'Regan, can I speak with you for a minute?'

Regan stood immediately. 'Yes, Miss Biggs.' She smirked to her classmates, and followed her out of the room.

Once Miss Biggs had left, Dru leaned over to Kal and whispered, 'I knew it! The dental check was a cover – they implanted everyone with something that lets them spy on all of us.'

Kal thought this through before whispering back. 'Does that mean I've got two implants, and I'm on the system twice?' he asked.

Dru nodded. 'I think so, and it means I'm unlisted.'

The two boys looked around the room at their classmates, terrified as the reality of what they'd learned sunk in. What did this mean for the children who were listed on the Infinity Group database?

CHAPTER **SEVEN**

'Wherever you go, you're being tracked for both of us,' said Dru, still trying to make sense of the information they'd gathered from Mr Park's computer.

'Which means we have to stay together,' said Kal.

Regan suddenly appeared in front of Dru and Kal, startling them as they made their way on foot to an Indian supermarket near to their house. 'What are you two talking about?' she said, trying but failing to look friendly.

Kal and Dru exchanged a suspicious look. 'Nothing,' responded Dru.

'What are you up to?' asked Regan.

'Waiting for our dadi,' answered Dru.

'Your what?'

'Our grandmother,' said Kal. 'We have some exciting grocery shopping to help her with. What do you want, Regan?'

Regan tried smiling. It didn't suit her. 'Oh, nothing. I just thought we could, like, hang out.'

The twins stared at her like she was crazy. Regan's smile began to falter, until . . .

'Here they are! My little wombats!' cried out Dadi as she sashayed towards them. 'Give your dadi a kiss.'

Regan stifled a giggle as Dadi grabbed Kal and Dru and kissed them. Dadi looked over at Regan. 'And you've brought a pretty school friend?'

'She's not a friend,' said Dru.

Regan put on a big grin. 'You're hilarious, Dru. We're, like, *best* friends, Mrs Dadi. I'm Regan.'

'Well, you want to come *desi* grocery shopping, Regan?' asked Dadi.

'Do I? Sure!' said Regan, full of enthusiasm.

Dadi flicked her sari purposefully and entered the Indian supermarket. Regan followed, leaving Kal and Dru glowering.

'What's she up to?' whispered Dru.

Kal shook his head. 'No idea.'

'Come along, boys,' called Dadi from inside the shop. The twins reluctantly followed.

Dadi pushed a trolley along the aisles of the supermarket, singing to herself, picking out various pickles and delicious chutneys. She grabbed a packet of baby *murukku* off the shelf, opened it and held one out to Regan. 'A little treat. Try it,' she said, eyes big.

Regan looked freaked out by the curled treats that resembled worms, but she took one and ate it, making a 'mm, yum!' face.

When Dadi returned to browsing the shelves, Regan spat it out. The twins exchanged a smile. Perhaps this was going to be more fun than they first thought.

'So, how are you feeling, Dru?' interrogated Regan.

'Fine,' answered Dru. 'Dadi, Regan wants to try some chilli banana chips too!'

Dadi was thrilled. 'Of course!' She opened a packet and popped one in Regan's mouth.

Regan grimaced. 'Mm. Delicious.'

Once she'd found her water bottle and swallowed most of the water in it, she returned to her interrogation. 'Did you two see who was on Mr Park's computer today?'

Dadi passed a tasting table, and stopped to try a few samples.

'Nah, no idea,' answered Kal. 'Dadi, do you think Regan would like some of that *nimbu* pickle too?'

'Good idea, my little wombats,' said Dadi. She prepared a sample and handed it to Regan.

Regan held up a hand, clearly ready to admit the boys had won this round. She sighed. 'I've got to go. Don't forget to keep an eye open, like Miss Biggs said.'

As Regan turned to leave, Kal said: 'Have you heard from Tim Hale?'

Regan screwed up her face. 'Why would I talk to that loser?' she said dismissively and bounced off.

Dadi turned to her grandsons. 'What an awful little girl.'

The twins couldn't have agreed more. Awful, and possibly dangerous too.

•

Later that afternoon Kal was sitting on his bed, typing on his laptop when Dru walked in clutching two old walkie-talkies.

'Hey, listen to this,' Kal said. '*Infinity Group is a philanthropic foundation aiming to enhance healthcare and reduce extreme poverty.*'

Dru rolled his eyes. 'Yeah, right.'

'What does philanthropic mean?' asked Kal. He knew his brother was a human encyclopedia. There was no need to look it up online if Dru was nearby.

'It means it's like a charity. The group has been set up to help society . . . supposedly,' said Dru.

Kal nodded. 'Look at this woman.' Kal showed Dru a corporate headshot of a well-groomed, wealthy-looking woman who appeared to be in her forties.

'She's Emma Ainsworth, and seems to be the brains behind Infinity Group. She's a billionaire, and she's got, like, twenty other billionaires chucking in money.'

Dru pointed at the screen. 'These are the people who are funding the Global Child Initiative. It's all part of Infinity Group.'

Kal nodded. 'Maybe it's not as bad as we think. Maybe they really are just trying to check up on kids' health.'

'Then why are they keeping it a secret?' Dru retorted. 'And what's with the weird side effects?'

They were good questions and ones that neither twin had an answer for.

Kal nodded towards the walkie-talkies. 'What have you got there? I thought we got rid of them years ago.'

'I've modified them for wider range,' answered Dru.

Kal scoffed. 'But we have mobile phones. And, we're not eight years old anymore.'

'Phones can be hacked. We don't want people listening to our conversations, hijacking the camera or tracking us.'

'But they're already tracking us.'

'No, they're tracking *you*,' corrected Dru. 'Everywhere you go, they think I'm with you. If they crosscheck with our mobiles and find out we're not really together –'

'– they'll know you're unlisted,' finished Kal.

'Exactly. We need to test the range. Feel like going for a ride?' asked Dru.

Kal didn't need to be asked twice. Anything to avoid doing maths homework, which he hadn't quite got around to doing yet anyway.

He ran downstairs, taking two steps at a time as usual. 'Just going for a ride, Dadi. Back soon!' he shouted as he grabbed his helmet and headed out the door.

'Make sure you're back in time for dinner, *beta*,' replied Dadi, cooking up a storm in the kitchen.

Dru remained in their bedroom as Kal sped down the street. After a few seconds, Dru turned on his walkie-talkie.

'Breaker breaker, this is kilo alpha lima, over,' said Kal, messing around.

Dru rolled his eyes at his brother's lame humour. 'Where are you now?'

'I'm just coming up to Tim's house. Wait, there's a –'

'There's a what?' Dru prompted, his heart rate suddenly increasing.

'There's a black van parked in Tim's driveway. Hang on . . . there's someone at the house. I'm gonna check it out.'

Dru was immediately concerned. 'No, Kal. It's too dangerous.' Over the walkie Kal replied, 'Don't worry, I'll be careful.'

'Kal? Kal, come in? Ugh, kilo alpha lima, this is delta romeo uniform, over?' said Dru, but received no response from his brother.

'I'm here,' Kal replied in a stage whisper. 'I'm next to the van . . . just going to have a little look through the window.'

Dru heard a shrill alarm and spun around in confusion – and then realised it was the van's alarm, which Kal had obviously set off.

'Kal!' he shouted into his handset. 'Kal?'

Long seconds passed until he heard the crackle of the walkie-talkie. 'It's okay, I'm here,' Kal panted. 'But Dru, I'm being followed.'

Dru wasn't sure he'd heard right. 'Kal?'

'Hang on, I'm gonna try to lose them.'

Dru could do nothing but wait, willing his brother to stay safe.

There was a crackle of static from the walkie-talkie. A new voice took over the airwave. 'Supermarket dumpster win! Sausages, tomatoes, chocolate.'

Another unknown voice responded. 'We saw a security guard. Do you think he was working for Infinity Group? Over.'

Kal's voice – he was clearly puffed, riding as hard as he could – came back over. 'What was that? Dru? Dru?'

Dru winced, relieved to hear Kal's voice but at the same time wanting him to stop talking. 'Quiet, Kal! Someone else is on our frequency.'

'I'm almost home,' responded Kal, missing his brother's warning, 'I've just turned into our street.' Dru rushed to their bedroom window and saw Kal speed onto the front lawn then dump his bike and duck behind a bush. Seconds later a black van cruised down the street.

'Okay, I'm safe,' panted Kal through the walkie-talkie.

Again, there was an unknown voice. 'Rose, did you hear that? Over.'

Someone else responded angrily. 'Shut up! Go to radio *silence*.'

Kal burst into the bedroom a moment later. 'Did you hear? Who was it?'

Dru turned off the walkie-talkie. 'I don't know, but I think we need to find out.'

CHAPTER EIGHT

Under the city, beneath St James train station was a network of connected tunnels that funnelled in, out and around the moving trains. The runaways had found a room of sorts to make a temporary base among the cavernous ceilings and dank soot coloured walls. It was damp and dark and miserable, but it was spacious and, for now, it was home. There were abandoned oil drums, milk crates for chairs and old wooden spindles that had once had cables wrapped around them, but were now being used for tables. A dirty slatted window looked out to another tunnel, where they could hear and see trains rattle by at regular intervals, headlights shining throughout the day and night. In the corner lay a pile of discarded white jumpsuits.

Kymara, thanks to the charity-bin haul earlier in the day, was wearing an old red corduroy jacket and a tourist cap with the word 'Santorini' on it. She fiddled with an old walkie-talkie.

Gemma, trying to wipe her glasses clean for the thirtieth time that day, wore a floral shirt with a T-shirt over the top of it, looking like an eighties throwback.

Rose and Jacob ran in, breathless, clutching a second walkie-talkie. They too had changed out of their jumpsuits into the clothing they'd found in the donations bin. Rose wore khaki army pants and a cream top, while Jacob blended into the dark background with a nondescript grey jacket and brown trousers.

Kymara looked up at them, worry etched on her face. 'Do you think they know who we are?' she asked, holding up the walkie-talkie.

Rose shrugged, looking unsure. But also concerned.

'They sounded around our age,' said Jacob.

Gemma shrugged. 'That doesn't mean it's not a trap.'

Back at the Sharma household, the twins were holding a similar debate.

'But what if it's not a trap? What if they're in trouble?' suggested Dru. He turned the walkie-talkie back on, and both boys listened to the crackle of radio silence. Dru took a deep breath, and raised the walkie-talkie to his mouth. 'Hello? Can you tell us who you are? Rose?'

In the tunnels, Rose glared at Kymara. 'I told you not to use our names over the radio!' she whispered.

Kymara mouthed, 'Sorry.'

Dru tried again. 'This isn't a trap.'

Kal shook his head. 'Dude, that's *exactly* what someone laying a trap would say.'

'We're as scared as you are,' he said into the handset. 'Weird stuff's happening, and I think you might know something about it.'

In the tunnels, the four teens looked at each other,

uncertain. 'It's safest to ignore them,' said Rose.

Gemma agreed. 'We have no idea who they are.'

Dru tried again. 'My name's Dru. What's yours?'

Kal was not impressed by his brother's honesty. 'Why would you tell them your name?!'

'We need them to trust us,' explained Dru.

In the tunnels, Jacob was desperate to make a connection with someone on the outside. 'I think it's legit,' he offered. 'They were being chased.'

In the twins' bedroom, there was only silence from the walkie-talkie. 'You've blown it,' Kal huffed, grabbing the walkie-talkie, ready to turn it off, when Rose spoke up. 'Why are you on this frequency?'

Dru grabbed the walkie-talkie back from his brother. 'We can't use our mobiles. They might be tracking them.'

In the tunnels, Kymara was nodding. 'That's my kind of paranoid.'

Rose responded on the handset, 'Who's they?'

There was silence for a moment, before the voice answered. 'Infinity Group.'

The runaways looked at each other, then Rose spoke. 'Is that who was chasing you?'

The voice replied: 'We think so. Yes.'

Kymara looked around at the others. 'They're like us,' she said, feeling hope for the first time in days.

Back at the Sharma household, the twins' sister, Vidya, stuck her head into their bedroom. 'Hey guys, it's time for –' Vidya stopped, and narrowed her eyes suspiciously. 'What are you two up to?'

Dru hid the walkie-talkie behind his back. 'Nothing.'

'What's behind your back?' she asked.

'None of your business. You ever heard of privacy?' asked Kal.

'You ever heard of acting suspiciously,' countered Vidya.

Kal stood up, ushering Vidya out. 'Get out, out. This is our bedroom.'

Kal slammed the door behind her, but Vidya wasn't finished. 'Well, it's dinner time!' she shouted through the door. 'And I'm going to find out what you're up to!' They heard her angry feet as she stamped down the stairs.

'How about we meet up tomorrow at Observatory Hill? It's central and easy to find,' the voice who called himself Dru, said.

'Wear a red hat,' suggested Rose over the walkie-talkie.

'Can it be a green hat?' Dru asked. 'I don't have a red one.'

Rose rolled her eyes at the other runaways, causing them to giggle. 'Fine. A green hat.'

'Okay, um . . . good talk. Over and out.'

Rose put down the walkie-talkie, and looked at the others. 'Okay everyone, I have a plan.'

•

As the Sharma twins headed down to dinner, Dru said to his brother, 'I hope we're not making a mistake.'

The teens in the tunnel were hoping the same thing. Regardless, each one of them felt a little less alone in the world after the conversation, and in this strange new world, this connection felt more important than ever.

•

Early the next morning, the streets of inner-city Sydney were relatively quiet. At seven o'clock it wasn't peak hour yet but there were still buses lining up to let eager workers start their days. Rose, Jacob and Gemma, hoodies covering their faces, walked through the city streets, trying hard not to draw attention to themselves.

There were already cafes open selling coffee and muffins, and the sight and smell almost brought tears to the eyes of the hungry teens. Breakfast used to be so easy – it was just there in the fridge waiting. But now, with no fridge and no money, simple things like food had got a lot more complicated.

Rose moved ahead of Jacob and Gemma, carrying a small map, on which she carefully marked with a red pen any place she saw a surveillance camera. Life would be so much easier if they could use mobiles but they had to survive off the grid, old school. At a street corner, she surreptitiously gestured behind her, towards a park across the street, which was camera-free. Gemma and Jacob hurried across the road to check out the park while Rose headed towards a secluded laneway a few metres away, head down.

Gemma and Jacob split up once they entered the park. Jacob started jogging, checking out the situation. There was a man wearing a suit on a bench, reading a newspaper. Next to him was a cup of hot coffee that smelled delicious, and a lunchbox. Jacob ran past the man, circled back behind him, then grabbed the lunchbox and sprinted away.

In the laneway, Rose stopped by a pile of flattened cardboard boxes. She picked a couple up but dropped them as a crawling mass of cockroaches scattered from underneath them. She stared at them, grossed out, and reconsidered. She knew the boxes would come in handy.

Back at the park, Jacob joined Gemma at a barbecue area. 'I got a lunchbox. I got a lunchbox!' said Jacob.

Gemma was collecting abandoned bottles and picnic litter. 'Oh look, aren't these pretty?' Her face lit up as she spotted a flowering bush. She began to pick the yellow flowers, but Jacob tapped her shoulder. 'We have to leave.'

Gemma looked up to see an angry man striding towards Jacob.

'Now!' reiterated Jacob, and the two sprinted towards the exit.

'Come back, thief!' yelled the man as the teens disappeared out of sight.

Back on the main road, they reunited with Rose. Together, the three headed for 'home', slipping through the iron gates back into the dark.

'This is going to get tired. Fast,' said Gemma as they spent a moment letting their eyes adjust to the dark before they started down the tunnel to their base.

'What took you so long?!' said Kymara, jumping out from an alcove in front of them, looking anxious. It wasn't the response the others were expecting.

Something more along the lines of: *Thanks for risking your lives so we could have breakfast* would have been appreciated.

'I don't like being alone, I told you that,' explained Kymara. 'I feel totally non-existent here.'

Rose was annoyed. 'Sh.'

'Don't "sh" me. You're the one who smashed my phone.'

''Cause you were posting,' argued Rose.

'But it's what I *do*,' countered Kymara.

Rose was unapologetic. 'Not anymore.'

Jacob held up a hand. 'We've gone through this,' he said calmly. 'They can track mobiles –'

'I know. I know,' said Kymara. 'But you could at least let me come out with you.'

'You're too recognisable,' explained Jacob.

Kymara shrugged, letting the hint of a grin be seen under her cap. 'I guess that's the price of fame.'

Rose and Jacob shared an eye roll as they headed back to their base.

Gemma, who had stayed quiet during the

heated exchange, gave Kymara the small bunch of handpicked flowers she'd been holding. 'I brought you something.'

'Thanks, Gemma,' said Kymara, touched by the gesture. She sniffed the flowers. 'They smell like fresh air.'

As the teens moved further into the tunnel, a siren went off. Jacob, Gemma and Rose ducked for cover, but Kymara stayed upright and chilled. 'Oh, I forgot to tell you: I set up an electronic sensor, we just triggered it walking in.'

'I just lost ten years of my life,' said Jacob, clutching his heart.

Rose was looking around. 'How'd you put it together?'

'Bits and pieces I found around the tunnels.' Kymara was proud and looked to Rose for approval.

'Cool. Nice work,' replied Rose with a nod.

They continued through the tunnels until they reached their base, where Jacob and Rose started to unpack their bags.

'So, what did you score?' asked Kymara. 'Apart from literal rubbish,' she added, looking at Rose's cardboard.

'I'm gonna sleep like a baby on these,' said Rose smugly.

'And I'm going to eat like a king,' said Jacob as he opened his lunchbox to find . . . a vegemite sandwich and a bag of potato chips. He almost cried at the sight. 'Why would anyone choose such a boring lunch?!'

'Who cares. I'm starving,' said Gemma, swiping at the chips.

Rose stopped her. 'Nice try. But we ration.' She moved to add the food to their stash, frowning. 'There's stuff missing.'

She eyeballed everyone, and stopped at Gemma.

'Don't look at me. Kymara's the one who's been here alone.'

'I didn't touch it,' answered Kymara. Then she pointed to Jacob. 'He's the one obsessed with food!'

'Hey,' said Jacob, hurt by the accusation.

'Okay, okay,' said Rose, as she ripped the sandwich into four portions and handed them out. 'I know we're all tired and hungry. But we'll never make it if we don't work as a team. Especially when we meet the walkie-talkie kids.' She looked at each of them. 'Are we good?'

The other three nodded, and bit into their pieces of sandwich.

Jacob howled with outrage. 'Noooo. It doesn't even have butter!'

CHAPTER NINE

Dru and Kal's morning started differently to that of the teens hiding out in the tunnels. For one, breakfast was drowning in butter, thanks to Dadi's attitude towards food in general. 'Put more butter on it, Vidya. It's good for your skin.'

Vidya protested. 'But the parathas are already cooked in ghee!'

'More grease, more love,' smiled Dadi. 'That's what your great-grandmother used to say.'

'No wonder she had a heart attack,' said Anousha under her breath.

'I heard that,' said Dadi, eyes flashing at her daughter-in-law. She looked over at the twins, who were whispering to each other. 'What are you two up to? No secrets.'

Dru looked guilty. 'We . . . we were talking about school.'

Dadi nodded. 'Ah, you must be gossiping about Multicultural Day, yes?'

Rahul groaned. 'Another special day.' He reached for his wallet. 'How much is this one going to cost, boys?'

'No money needed,' explained Dadi. 'The Global Child Initiative is covering everything.'

Rahul sat back, pleased. 'Not going to argue with that.'

Dadi handed out more parathas to the family. 'And the boys' rockstar dadi is going to teach the kiddies the ancient sport of *kabaddi*.'

Anousha looked at the boys and then back to Dadi, alarmed. 'Isn't that a bit brutal for school?'

Dadi's eyes sparkled. 'Exactly! They won't know what hit them. Literally!'

Anousha turned to her husband with her eyebrows raised. Rahul, his mouth full of delicious paratha, looked too content to worry about unleashing his mother on an unsuspecting school community.

After Dadi had given the boys *badams* – soaked almonds – for added strength, they were excused from the breakfast table.

Back in their bedroom, the boys stood in front of Dru's open wardrobe door. Stuck on it was the outline of a chart that Dru had drawn to map what they'd found out so far about Infinity and the dental check. He had a pad of Post-it notes ready to begin. 'So, what do we know?'

Kal was less interested. 'It looks like a year five project. Can't we do this on your iPad?'

Dru shook his head. 'It's not secure. Come on, it will be kind of fun.'

Kal disagreed. 'This is why you and I will never be friends.'

Dru ignored his brother's lack of enthusiasm and started writing on the Post-it notes and sticking them to the chart. *'Tracking started after the dentist check.' 'The Global Child Initiative is funded by Infinity Group.'*

Kal moved to his bed, grabbed a tennis ball and started throwing it up in the air. 'The only thing that matters right now is finding Tim,' he said stubbornly.

'We can't do that until we know where to look,' said Dru, adding another Post-it to the chart. *'Tim and his parents. Missing.'*

Frustrated, Kal threw the ball and it hit the ceiling hard. So hard, in fact, that it got lodged there. Both boys looked at the ceiling in shared alarm.

Dadi called out from outside the bedroom, 'Are you two practising kabaddi without me?'

'No, Dadi,' said Dru as he wrote on another Post-it note. *'Kal shows signs of insane super strength.'*

Dru knew that Kal felt a little proud of his strength, even though he had no idea why he'd been given it. His brother's self-satisfied smile was a giveaway. 'How are you going to explain that' – he pointed to the ball in the ceiling – 'to Mum?'

Kal shrugged it off. 'She won't even notice. Anyway,

enough of that; we need to get to school.'

Dru sometimes wished he had a tenth of his brother's laid-back attitude. There were always a hundred things whizzing around his brain, causing concern. And with all that was going on with Infinity Group, the hundred things had multiplied by ten at least. Dru shut the wardrobe door with a bang.

•

On the bike ride in, Dru kept on thinking. He tried to talk to Kal but his brother sped ahead. 'Slow down, we need to talk!' he yelled.

'Sorry, can't hear you,' said Kal.

'It's about you,' tried Dru.

Bingo. Kal slowed and waited for his brother to catch up.

'You've got two implants, right? So, maybe you're twice as strong as other kids.'

'Awesome,' said Kal.

Dru shook his head. 'Not if it gets us caught. You've got to control it.'

Kal remained cocky. 'What can I say? I don't know my own strength.'

'Exactly,' replied Dru. 'Follow me.' Dru turned in a different direction from school, with Kal right on his tail.

•

The abandoned metal wreckers near the harbour looked like it hadn't been used for years, and was littered with metal scraps of different shapes and sizes. The perfect location for testing strength.

Kal started by lifting a rusted metal chest. 'Too easy,' he bragged to Dru.

Next he moved on to a large roll of wire fencing. He struggled to get his hands around it but once he had, he lifted it with ease.

Kal looked around for something that would really stretch his newfound ability, and his eyes landed on a rusted-out car.

Dru saw where his brother was looking. 'Don't even think about it, Kal.' But it was too late. Kal had thought about it. He jogged over and did a few cursory squats to warm up his quadriceps, groaned a bit and then, amazingly, lifted the car off the ground with his bare hands.

'Are you for real?' asked Dru.

Kal grinned and then dropped the car suddenly.

'Careful, we don't want to draw attention –'

'Too late,' interrupted Kal.

Dru spun around to see a security guard striding over to the boys. 'Oi, you two. What are you doing?' she shouted gruffly.

The boys ran off, with Kal sprinting far ahead. Dru followed as fast as he could but the security guard was fit, and gaining on him.

Dru ducked into one of the rows of metal scraps to his left. It provided a better chance of not getting caught than trying to outrun the guard. He was scared, panting heavily, crouched down behind a rusty washing machine. Had the guard actually seen Kal lifting up the car? How would they explain their way out of this?

Up ahead, Kal stopped and saw the security guard

about to run towards the scrap lanes after Dru. He shouted out, 'Hey, lady!'

The guard looked up and took the bait. She started sprinting towards Kal. Before Kal took off, he saw Dru making his escape through a hole in the side fence. Then Kal accelerated and easily outran the security guard, jumping over a wire fence and doubling back to where the twins had left their bikes.

Dru was waiting for him. 'We've got ten minutes to get to school.'

Kal grinned. 'Race you!' He jumped on his bike and took off.

Dru groaned and pedalled after him.

CHAPTER TEN

The boys walked through the school gymnasium, backpacks on, just as the school bell rang. The glass doors that looked out on the oval were open wide. The area overflowed with people. Both the hall and the outdoor area was already covered with Multicultural Day stalls and activities. There was a tai chi demonstration, a capoeira lesson, Irish dancing, and food stalls, with kids dressed in their cultural costumes. The twins wore their sports uniforms.

Kal looked around him, impressed. 'This *so* beats being stuck in class.'

The twins walked past the capoeira class. Various students moved through the poses with power and precision. Miss Biggs was nearby, watching closely.

'Why is Miss Biggs taking notes?' asked Dru with a frown.

Kal shrugged. 'Who knows why Nurse Frankenstein does anything.'

The twins chuckled. 'Hey, thanks for getting that security guard off my tail,' said Dru a little sheepishly.

'No probs,' replied Kal. 'Did you see me lift that car?'

Dru nodded. 'Yeah. It was pretty sick.'

They saw Dadi up ahead. She had left home an hour before them to set up, next to the kabaddi court that had been chalked for the occasion. She was pumped, loudspeaker in hand, ready to drum up support for one of India's favourite sports. Chloe was already by her side, calling her friends to join the fun.

Dadi waved the boys over and spoke into her loudspeaker. 'Hurry up. Let's get ready to rumble!'

'What fool gave her a loudspeaker?' laughed Kal.

Dadi had a competitive spirit second to none, and she was looking even more amped than usual. She wanted more players and more of an audience. 'Come one, come all!' she yelled into the loudspeaker. 'And join in the sport that's the ultimate test of endurance!'

Dru sidled up to Chloe with a shy smile. 'Are you going to have a go?'

Chloe grinned. 'Totally. I'm feeling especially fit at the moment. Must be something in the water.'

Dru shifted uncomfortably, but Chloe didn't notice.

'Hey, did you find out anything more about what happened to Kymara? She still hasn't posted anything.'

Dru frowned. 'Not yet, but I'm working on it.'

Regan and a friend strode past the kabaddi court, heading for the Irish dancing display.

'Regan!' Dadi called via the loudspeaker. 'I remember you. Back over here. Don't bother with that dancing rubbish. They don't even use their arms!'

Amused, Regan stopped. 'Hi, Mrs Dadi.'

Dadi looked around the assembled group, clearly pleased by the growing numbers. 'Welcome to kabaddi,' she began. 'The rules are simple. There are two teams, on opposite sides of the court. A player from one team has to enter the opposition's side and tag as many kids out as possible. One kid equals one point.'

Regan turned to her friend and whispered, 'Yawn!'

Dadi looked directly at Regan and frowned. 'Nothing boring about getting slammed to the ground!' she shouted. 'Speaking of which, the opposition must tackle the player, and stop them from getting back to their side.'

Kal was looking around as students gathered around the kabaddi court. 'Tim would've loved this.'

Dru nodded. 'Don't worry. We'll find him.'

Dadi continued her explanation over the loudspeaker. 'And the most vital part – the player must chant, "kabaddi, kabaddi, kabaddi!" The second they stop, they are out.'

Dru couldn't help but grin. 'Dadi sure knows how to sell the game.'

Dadi smiled at her grandsons. 'My little wombats will be the captains of the first round.'

Regan laughed out loud. 'Little *wombats*.'

Dru grimaced. 'This is going to be painful in more ways than one,' he said to his brother.

'At least Dadi cheers you on. She always ignores me,' said Kal.

'Not true,' countered Dru.

Through the loudspeaker Dadi called, 'Let's do this! Come on, Dru!'

Kal looked at Dru. 'Told you.'

Kal took his place on one side of the court, with six teammates. Dru stepped up, and started chanting. 'Kabaddi, kabaddi, kabaddi . . .'

He continued chanting as he attempted to tag the opposition.

Chloe called out from the sidelines. 'You've got this!'

Dru threw himself into the pack, but the other players were too fast for him. They bounced around, super lithe and fit.

Dru tried to tag the smallest player but even he dodged out of the way.

Over the loudspeaker, Dadi's competitive spirit took flight. 'Come on, Dru. Fight!'

A couple of the teachers walking around the gymnasium looked over at Dadi, a little thrown by the loud grandmother with the loudspeaker.

Before Dru could do anything else, Kal launched for his brother and pinned him down with ease. Out of breath, Dru stopped his chant.

Into the loudspeaker, Dadi called it. 'And he's out for this round!'

Disappointed, a squashed Dru looked over at Chloe and Dadi.

Another member of Dru's team, Xavier, who was tall and stocky and up for a kabaddi challenge, began his charge. 'Kabaddi, kabaddi, kabaddi!' But he barely got a metre into the opposing side's space before Kal leapt towards him and tackled him to the ground.

'That's the Sharma spirit!' Dadi yelled, clearly thrilled.

Xavier tried to wriggle free, feebly shouting, 'Kabaddi, kabaddi,' but he gave up when it was clear Kal had the upper hand.

'And Kal Sharma does it again!' yelled Dadi.

Kal threw his hands up in the air, a beaming smile on his face.

Dru looked over at Regan, who was watching Kal with interest. A whistle blew and Dadi spoke over the loudspeaker, 'Time for a water break. Hydrate, but don't make me wait.'

Dru moved over to Kal. 'What are you doing?' he asked, annoyed.

'Smashing it!' said Kal with a triumphant grin.

'Kal, pull it back,' warned Dru. 'You're gonna get us busted.'

'Relax, it would be weirder if I wasn't demolishing you,' said Kal, chugging down water from his water bottle.

Regan moved over to the twins. 'Have you been working out, Sharma?' she asked Kal.

'Yeah, I have,' answered Kal. When it was clear that

was the end of the conversation, Regan moved off.

'See what I mean,' said Dru. 'No-one can find out what's going on. Especially not Regan, she is always such a busybody.'

'But Dadi's actually proud of me. That never happens. What do you want me to do?' asked Kal.

'You have to throw the match,' said Dru.

Kal gave a sarcastic laugh. 'Oh sure, so you can look good?'

Dru shook his head, and said quietly, 'No, so I don't get taken. Like Tim and his parents did.'

Kal sobered up at the mention of his missing friend. He headed back to the court.

Dadi, unaware of the tension between the twins, was loving every minute of the game. 'The mood is tense as my little wombat steps up as the final raider for his team. To win, he must tag five opponents and make it back safely. Good luck to both my grandsons.'

Kal moved forwards and began his chant, 'Kabaddi, kabaddi, kabaddi . . .'

Dru and his team circled around Kal. But Kal

manoeuvered through them as he easily tagged – one, two, three, four players.

'Yes! He's got four!' shouted Dadi. 'Only one more needed for the win.'

Kal looked over at his brother, still chanting, 'Kabaddi, kabaddi, kabaddi . . .'

Dru, standing back, hoped Kal wouldn't go for him but a fired-up Kal headed straight in his direction until a strong kid, Zhang, intercepted Kal and tackled him.

'And he's captured!' Dadi shouted. Zhang pushed Kal back towards his side while Kal kept up the chant, 'Kabaddi, kabaddi, kabaddi . . .'

Regan sneered with her mates, and called out in a poor impersonation of Dadi's voice, 'Come on, *wombat*, don't stuff it up now.'

Dadi looked unimpressed and immediately shouted into the loudspeaker, 'Quiet on the court!'

But Regan had riled Kal, and he wasn't prepared to pretend he couldn't win. He used all his strength to flip Zhang off, and he went flying across the court. Onlookers gasped.

Kal then looked to Dru, and went for him. Dru held his position, willing his twin not to show any more super strength. *Don't do this. Please, bro!*

At the last moment Kal stopped in front of Dru, and fell to the ground, pretending he landed badly.

The crowd gasped again.

Dadi was spellbound by the action. 'And this is Dru's chance.'

Dru dropped on top of Kal, and held him down. Eventually Kal stopped chanting kabaddi and it was all over.

Dadi cheered. 'And Dru brings it home for his team!'

Dru's team cheered. As did Dadi and Chloe and the rest of the audience. Dru reached his hand out to help Kal up. 'Thank you,' he said quietly.

Dru saw that Kal was furious. Dru tried to reach for his brother's hand, but he stood up and sprinted off. Dru let him be for a minute and then made his way behind the toilet block, where he came across Kal standing over an aluminium garbage bin that had been crumpled like a tin can. But he wasn't looking at the bin; his eyes were following the back of Regan, who was running in the other direction.

'There you are.'

Dru continued. 'I know that wasn't easy. But our secret's safe. And that means we are too.'

Kal took a deep breath. 'Yep. Cool,' he said, avoiding eye contact with his twin.

CHAPTER **ELEVEN**

After school, back at the Sharma house, Dru and Kal were trying to convince their older sister to do them a favour. It wasn't going well.

'There's no way I'm covering for you,' said Vidya, sitting on the edge of Kal's bed.

'Pleeeease!' pleaded Dru.

Vidya stared at both her brothers. 'Why are you sneaking out at night anyway?'

'No reason,' said Dru.

'How dumb do you think I am?' asked Vidya.

Kal stepped forwards, playing earnest. 'Dru. It's

time to tell her –'

'No!' said Dru, seriously worried his brother was going to say something he shouldn't.

Kal tried to keep a straight face. 'We have girlfriends. And we're going on a double date.'

Vidya just laughed. 'Worst. Lie. Ever.'

Kal pulled a twenty-dollar note from his wallet. 'Have this, then.'

This was more like it. 'Make it fifty and we have a deal,' said their older sister.

Kal was outraged. 'I'm not made of cash. This is my birthday money!'

Vidya stood firm. 'Then it's a no go.'

'Or, is it?' said Kal, holding up his phone. He opened a video of Vidya dancing and singing a Bollywood song in the mirror in the bathroom, unaware she was being filmed by her dastardly brother.

'Nooooo,' she cried, knowing a video leak like that would harm her social media profile.

Kal continued to play tough. 'Help us. Or Dru will hack into your Instagram and post this for all of your followers to enjoy – all four of them.'

Vidya groaned. 'Fine. But I'm keeping this.' She swiped the twenty bucks from Kal's hand and left the bedroom.

Dru turned to Kal. 'You can't use my hacking as a threat.'

Kal shrugged. 'It worked, didn't it?'

Dru sighed. 'True.'

Minutes later they snuck down the stairs, pausing at the bottom to eavesdrop on the conversation in the kitchen. Rahul was prepping the vegetables for dinner and wasn't pleased about it. 'Where were you?' he asked Vidya grumpily.

'In my room, talking to –' she hesitated, considering her response. 'A mate on the phone.'

Dadi shook her head. 'You know the rules. Chore time means bore time. No phones.'

'Sorry, Dadi,' said Vidya, taking over the chopping from her dad.

Behind her, in the hallway, Dru and Kal crept out the front door.

•

Back at the tunnels Rose pulled on a backpack, getting ready to meet the boys at Observatory Hill. Gemma, Jacob and Kymara came up behind her.

'What's going on?' she asked.

'We've been talking about this meeting,' said Gemma, nominated as group spokesperson. 'We've changed our minds, we don't want to go. We're scared we are going to get caught '

'You're telling me *now*?' said Rose, annoyed.

'I tried to tell you before,' replied Gemma.

Rose looked past her to the others. 'And you all agree?'

Kymara said, 'We shouldn't do anything hasty.'

'Jacob?' prompted Rose.

'I reckon we'd be all right. But if we're not . . . and we get captured . . .' Jacob trailed off. At home Jacob was normally super laid-back. He was the peacemaker. When his two brothers fought, he was always there to smooth things over. He wished he was with them now. He wanted to support Rose but there was so much to lose if things went wrong. 'I just want to see my family again.'

Rose needed to think. She sat down, unsure about what was going to happen next. She had to come up with a foolproof plan that would make the others feel safe.

•

Dru and Kal were on edge as they rode through the suburban streets in the late afternoon.

'Maybe you shouldn't have come,' whispered Dru. 'They're tracking you. And these kids seriously don't want to be found.'

'It's way more dangerous for us to split up,' whispered Kal in reply. 'And you need me to save your butt if something goes wrong.' He looked around him before whispering again, 'Why are we whispering?'

Dru shrugged. 'I don't know, but it feels safer.'

The boys tried to keep to the shadows as they made their way to the train station, where they locked their bikes and helmets away and headed onto the train platform. They put on their green caps and tried not to freak out as they stood in a dark corner and watched the action around them.

'What do you think's going on?' asked Dru, nodding towards a boy about their age who was being questioned by two black-suited uniformed men on the platform opposite.

'Maybe he skimped on buying a ticket?' said Kal.

One of the men took out an iPad and started to type.

The boy looked around him, panicked, and suddenly ran. The men quickly gave chase.

Kal was shocked. 'What are you –' he called out before Dru grabbed his arm, motioning him to stop.

One of the men noticed Kal's outburst and started walking across the bridge to their platform. 'Hey! You two,' he called out to them.

Kal panicked. 'Run!'

Dru tried to remain practical. 'No – we can't miss the train.'

The man was now jogging down the steps onto the boys' platform when their train finally pulled in. The doors opened and Kal and Dru jumped on, scared. They pulled their hats down to hide their faces as the man rushed towards the door, seconds away from boarding the train. But he was too late. The whistle blew and the doors slammed shut.

The twins slumped down on seats, relieved the carriage was empty.

'I don't think that had anything to do with having a ticket, do you?' asked Dru.

Kal shook his head, despondent.

•

Back at the Sharma house Vidya was in her bedroom watching a Bollywood dance number on her iPad, when Dadi walked to the bottom of the stairs and called out to the boys. Vidya ran over to her. 'Hey, Dadi. What's up?' she said, putting an arm around Dadi's shoulders and turning her away from the stairs.

'Just calling the wombats to dinner,' said Dadi.

'Oh, they grabbed an early dinner and went to bed,' said Vidya.

Dadi looked incredulous. 'Bed? Already? I'll go check on them.'

'No, don't do that. I tried to chat with them and they were really cranky, because they were nearly asleep,' said Vidya. 'They said they were totally wiped out from today.'

Dadi began to nod. 'Makes sense. Kabaddi is very demanding.' She looked disappointed. 'But I had all of these new moves I wanted to show them after dinner. Oh well, I'll have to show you instead,' she said with a sparkle in her eye.

'Mm, great,' said Vidya between gritted teeth. Her brothers were most definitely going to pay for this.

•

Circular Quay train station was bustling, filled with tourists and people rushing home from work. Dru and Kal felt a lot safer when they emerged from the quiet of the train carriage and were surrounded by people. Once they moved away from the noise of the station, the crowds thinned out.

The twins entered the tunnel that led to Observatory Hill and continued on to the entrance of the park, coming to a stop at a heavy boom gate. Observatory Hill had a magnificent view of the harbour and was close to the Harbour Bridge. From this vantage point Sydney city looked postcard perfect. A sign saying 'Park Closes at 5.00 p.m.' was prominently displayed on the gate.

Dru consulted his watch. It was nearer seven.

'We've come this far,' said Kal.

The brothers moved silently over to the meeting spot. But no-one was there.

Dru looked at his watch. 'Looks like they're late.'

'Rude,' said Kal, making a joke.

Dusk was starting to fall and the boys positioned themselves in the shadow of a tree, so they were hidden from general view. Flying foxes screeched overhead, their heavy wings beating rhythmically as they passed by.

Suddenly a voice called out to them, 'Hey, park's closed.'

They looked over to where the shout had come from, and saw a park ranger in the near-dark. 'Stay here,' said Kal quietly. 'I'll distract him.' Before Dru could respond Kal ran over to where a bollard was attached to the ground. With incredible strength he ripped it from the ground and hurled it down the hill. The guard ran off in the direction of the noise, and Kal ran back to Dru.

'Did you see that?' He was still buzzed by his amazing strength.

'Even better than lifting the car,' said Dru.

Kal looked around. 'So, where are these walkie-talkie kids?'

Dru shrugged.

'Maybe they were just messing with us.'

Dru could see that Kal wasn't impressed, and he too was about ready to give up. 'It's possible. Let's go home. I don't –'

He didn't get to finish the sentence, because a second later, hessian sacks were pulled over both boys' heads, and everything went black.

CHAPTER TWELVE

Dru tried hard not to panic.

'Get off me!' he yelled, but the hessian sack remained tight. To Dru it smelled like the cupboard under the kitchen sink, where Dadi kept a big bag of potatoes. He stopped struggling and tried to breathe lightly as he listened to the sounds around him. People scuffling, possibly fighting, followed by a groan. The person holding on to him loosened their grip for a moment and Dru was able to push away and remove the sack from his head.

It took a few moments for his eyes to adjust to the

light. He was outdoors, and in front of him was Kal, still hooded and fighting against four teenagers. His arms were flailing and they were fighting to keep him contained. But the group wasn't prepared for Kal's strength. One by one the teens went flying. Kal ran over to Dru, and they stood staring at three girls and a boy all sprawled on the ground, groaning.

Kal looked furious. 'Let's get out of here. *Now*,' he said.

'Wait,' said Dru, then turned to the teens. 'Why did you attack us?'

'We weren't attacking you,' said Gemma, rubbing her arm gingerly.

'We were trying to take you to our hide-out,' explained Rose, slowly getting to her feet.

'But we needed to use the sacks to make sure you didn't know where we were taking you,' added Kymara.

Dru looked over at the girl standing up. 'You're Rose?' he asked. He tried not to blush. She was Filipino and pretty, with intense eyes.

She nodded. Dru could tell there was fear behind her bravado. Kal wasn't interested in getting to know anyone right now. 'So, you *were* kidnapping us,' he said accusingly.

Rose moved over to Jacob, who was clutching his leg. 'You okay, Jacob?' she asked.

'Landed on something metal or something,' he replied.

In the faint light Rose took a close look at Jacob's leg. His calf was bleeding and there was a nasty gash. She helped him to his feet as Kymara and Gemma made their way over to Rose and Jacob.

'This was a mistake,' Gemma said.

Kal agreed. 'Yeah. A big mistake.'

'Let's go,' said Kymara.

Dru looked closely at her. She was tall, Indigenous, and very familiar-looking. 'Hang on a minute: you're Kymara Russell. People are looking for you.'

Kymara looked panicked. 'And now we *really* need to go.'

The four teens started to head off, but Dru called

out after them. 'Wait. What do you know about Infinity Group?'

Rose turned back. 'You can't talk about that out here! It's not safe.'

Dru looked at Kal quickly and then called out, 'Okay, then I'll come to your hide-out.'

Kal looked incredulous. 'What?!'

The others stopped and looked at the twins. Dru said to Kal, 'We need them. We can't do this on our own.'

'*I* can. You saw what I did to them.'

Dru knew he only had seconds to save the situation. He spoke to Rose. 'My brother's being tracked – he has to stay here. But take me.'

Kymara frowned. 'Did he say "tracked"?'

Rose moved closer to the twins. 'Tracked by who?'

'If you're going, I'm coming with you,' said Kal.

Dru shook his head. 'We can't risk leaving a trail to their hide-out.' He turned to the others. 'Can one of you wait with Kal so he knows you'll bring me back?'

Rose nodded. 'I'll stay. But you'll have to start giving us some answers.'

Gemma wasn't happy with the direction the conversation was taking. 'You can't be serious?'

'Take him to the hide-out,' instructed Rose. 'He's right, we have no other option. We need to work together.'

'Stay out of sight of the park ranger,' warned Dru.

Jacob looked between Gemma and Rose and came to a decision. 'Okay. But I'll stick with him,' he said, pointing to Kal. 'Wouldn't mind sitting down, plus I can take on Mr Muscles if I have to.'

Kal laughed. 'You reckon?'

The kids all looked at each other, united in their uncertainty. Were they going to be able to trust one another?

•

Back inside the tunnels, Gemma, Kymara and Rose led Dru, who was once again wearing the hessian sack, through the darkness, past ancient graffiti and mysterious side passages. Dru could hear the echoes of subterranean drips, faraway roadworks and rumbling underground trains as he stumbled along.

Kymara, slightly ahead of the group, called out, 'Stop.'

The others stopped and Dru banged his knee. 'Ow.'

Kymara ducked down and pulled a fine rope at ankle height, disarming one of her booby traps before continuing. 'Okay. Bring him through.'

'Lift your foot,' said Rose.

Dru followed the instruction. 'Now your other one,' added Rose. He did as he was told, and they continued past the trip-wire.

Once everyone had gone ahead, Kymara rearmed the wire.

'Are we underground?' asked Dru.

'Don't worry about where we are,' answered Rose, gruffly.

'This is a bad idea,' Gemma said nervously. 'He's gonna get us caught.'

Dru felt something scamper across one of his feet. 'Argh. What was that?'

Kymara answered dryly: 'Either a rat or a cockroach.'

'It was big,' said Dru.

'Cockroach, then,' replied Kymara with a laugh. 'Come on.'

•

Meanwhile, above ground, Kal had no trouble keeping pace with a limping Jacob. But he wasn't ready to trust him yet. 'You better not be leading me into something,' he warned. The backdrop of the city buildings contrasted with the harbour outlook on top of the hill. For a second as the two boys looked at the beautiful lights as they twinkled across the harbour and they could forget why they were there.

'Chill, bro,' replied Jacob. 'There's a spot where we can hide up ahead.'

The boys spotted the park ranger a short distance away and started to run. But Jacob was slow.

'Come on,' Kal said to Jacob.

Jacob struggled, limping. 'I'm trying.'

Kal realised he'd have to help the boy if they were to both get away safely. He went back to Jacob and put an arm around him.

'What are you doing?' asked Jacob, feeling awkward but knowing he needed assistance.

Kal half-carried the injured boy away at speed. 'Is it straight ahead?' asked Kal.

Jacob pointed a short distance away. 'Down that slope.'

The pair headed towards the side of a hill, and came to a halt near a large tree that overlooked the harbour. Kal helped Jacob settle inside the exposed twisted roots, and the two boys caught their breath.

Kal looked behind the tree. There was no sign of the ranger. 'Think we've lost him.'

'Totally coulda done that without your help,' said Jacob as he clutched his injured calf, wincing.

Kal rolled his eyes. 'Totally.'

They stared out at Luna Park across the harbour – the Ferris wheel all lit up. It was weird to think that people were there enjoying themselves. Kal opened up his backpack. Jacob tensed, knowing he was vulnerable but trying to appear tough.

Kal pulled out a tiffin, a round silver container, filled with samosas, and bit into one.

Jacob looked away, attempting to look uninterested, but he couldn't help sneaking glances as Kal ate. The samosa's aroma was tickling his nostrils and his salivary glands started up. It was even more painful than his injured calf. His stomach rumbled.

Kal couldn't not have missed hearing the rumble but callously kept chewing. Then, relenting, he pulled a second samosa from his bag and offered it to Jacob. Jacob looked at it warily.

'Go on,' said Kal. 'It's good.'

Jacob couldn't resist a moment longer. He bit into it and groaned with pleasure. Kal laughed at the boy's over-the-top reaction.

'My grandmother's samosa,' said Kal, with a hint of pride.

Jacob's blissful expression moved to sadness in an

instant. 'I miss my mum's cooking,' he said. 'Haven't seen her since this whole thing started.'

'It must suck, being away from your family. Why do you think people are after you?' said Kal.

'I just have no idea what's going on. They picked us up in vans, held us in a big hall and they were moving us, I don't know where to. It feels like a nightmare. What do my family think's happened to me? Are they safe?' Jacob was finding it hard to stop the emotion from entering his voice.

'Things are pretty scary right now, eh,' said Kal sympathetically. He wished he had answers to Jacob's questions but he didn't.

Jacob nodded. 'Maybe we can help each other to figure this all out,' he suggested, licking his fingers, clean. 'You got any more?'

Kal laughed. 'Dude. I'm not a food truck.'

CHAPTER THIRTEEN

They led Dru through the tunnels, and as soon as Rose
felt they were far enough in, the hessian sack was removed
from Dru's head. He looked around, dumbfounded
by his surroundings. The group's subterranean tunnel
living area was spartan and uninviting. Water ran down
one of the harsh concrete walls. Old cans of drink and
discarded food wrappers were everywhere. There was a
makeshift washing line with some clothes hung up in
the corner. Old sleeping-bags and moth-eaten blankets
lay on flattened cardboard boxes. A couple of torches
lit the dark, dusty space.

'This is where you're hiding out?' asked Dru, unable to mask the distaste in his voice.

'Home sweet home,' said a sarcastic Kymara.

Dru couldn't help staring at her. 'I still can't believe you're Kymara Russell.'

'You've seen my posts?' asked Kymara. 'You a gamer?'

'We didn't go through all this for Kymara to meet her fans,' huffed Gemma.

Rose pulled up a milk crate for Dru to sit on. She sat facing him, interrogation-style. 'So, Dru is it? Tell us everything you know about Infinity Group.'

'Um . . . well, I hacked the system on my school's network,' started Dru, feeling a bit nervous. He wasn't great around people he didn't know anyway, and this was so far out of his comfort zone he was straining to keep it together.

Kymara grinned. 'A hacker too. Nice.'

Kymara gave Dru a fist bump.

'And I found out Infinity Group is behind the Global Child Initiative,' continued Dru.

'The Global Child Initiative came to my school,' said Rose. 'What do they want from us?'

'We don't know. But they're tracking kids. They did something during the compulsory dentist check. And it's making them super strong.'

Gemma raised an eyebrow. 'That would explain your brother's gorilla-like performance back at the park, then.'

Dru nodded. 'Yeah. Exactly. It's scary.'

The girls nodded in unison. It seemed they were all slowly beginning to trust each other.

'I took off from school because my dad was sick the day of the dentist check,' said Rose.

'One of Dad's farmhands was visiting family interstate, so I stayed home and helped Dad on the farm that day,' said Gemma wistfully.

They looked to Kymara for her explanation. 'I didn't need a reason. It's the dentist,' she said with a shrug.

Dru smiled. His nervousness was melting away. 'Same here.'

Under more normal circumstances, these two might have enjoyed being friends.

'That's probably why Infinity Group wants to find you,' says Dru. 'Because you all missed the dental check-up and weren't implanted.'

'What do you mean, "implanted"?' Rose asked.

'Kal took my place at the check-up, so he got two implants. We don't know exactly what the implant can do or what they look like. We just know they are slowly changing kids and that their movements are being recorded. He's being tracked for both of us. But I'm not and I guess you aren't either, you're all like me – unlisted.'

'And that means that we're being hunted?'

Dru nodded. 'This one kid we know, Tim Hale – made a run for it to avoid the dental check, and Infinity Group chased him down in a van.'

'Oh, we know the Infinity vans,' Kymara said with a grimace.

'We'd been rounded up, and the four of us were in one when it crashed,' explained Rose when she saw Dru's confused expression. 'That's how we escaped.'

'That kid, Tim,' said Gemma. 'What happened to his family?'

Dru saw three hopeful faces looking back at him. He didn't want to be the one to deliver more bad news, but he didn't want to lie to them either.

'His parents, er, were taken. But I don't know where or what's happened to them. Kal and I went back to their house and it's deserted. No sign of Tim or his parents.'

Rose and Kymara said nothing. Gemma stood up and walked away.

Dru tried to salvage the mood. 'But Tim's parents were against the dental check-up. It doesn't mean your families are . . . you know . . .'

Gemma was having none of it. 'We have no way of knowing if our families are okay. And bringing him here just puts us more at risk.'

Dru looked down, knowing that nothing he could say would make these girls feel better about their dire situation.

'Gemma's right,' said Rose. 'We better get you

out of here.' She grabbed the sack and moved closer to Dru.

He baulked. 'I don't need to wear that thing again, do I?'

'Yes, you do,' said Kymara. The other girls nodded their agreement.

Gemma threw the sack over his head.

Dru groaned but went with Rose as they trekked back through the labyrinth of tunnels. Rose paused to guide him over the trip-wire again.

They moved a little further, and after turning a corner she pulled the sack off his head. 'If we're going to survive, we'll need friends,' said Rose seriously. 'But you have to promise you won't tell anyone about us. Not one person.'

'I promise,' replied Dru, equally serious.

'You said your brother got two implants,' said Rose. 'Is he going to be a problem?'

'Don't worry about Kal,' said Dru. 'You can trust him.'

Dru and Rose reached the entrance to the tunnels.

'Be careful out there,' said Rose. 'I should warn you: when we were locked up, the ones in charge wore orange badges. Keep an eye out for them.' For the first time Dru could see Rose was close to tears.

Dru tried to comfort her. 'Thanks. Don't worry. It's going to be okay.'

Rose shrugged, a little bitter. 'Easy to say when you're going home to your family tonight.'

Dru could only nod.

•

At the base of the tree, Kal and Jacob were sitting in companionable silence until Kal decided to show Jacob one of his new tricks.

'Check this out,' he said, and picked up a rock and squeezed it until it exploded into dust.

'Whoa! That's sick!' exclaimed Jacob. And then, after a moment he said quietly, 'Why does Infinity want kids to be super strong? Isn't it kind of dangerous?'

'Maybe, but it's cool as well,' added Kal. He

dusted off his hand with his T-shirt, showing a glimpse of the Western Sydney Wanderers top he wore underneath.

Jacob noticed. 'Wanderers? All right.'

Jacob's response surprised Kal. 'You follow the Wanderers?'

'Who else is there?' asked Jacob.

'You're not so bad after all,' said Kal.

'Don't act so surprised,' said Jacob with a grin.

A whistle sounded a short distance away from them, making them both suddenly wary. 'Did you hear that?' Kal said.

Jacob nodded, relaxed, and whistled back.

Rose appeared a moment later, followed by Dru.

Kal stood up, trying to mask a yawn. He looked over to his brother. 'You okay?'

'I'm fine. These guys are unlisted, like me.'

'All good here?' Rose asked Jacob.

'I kept this fella under control,' replied Jacob with a grin, then winced as he stood up. Rose looked at his leg. 'It doesn't look great. We have to get you back.'

Dru took out one of the walkie-talkies from his backpack and offered it to Rose. 'Take this. I modified it to have longer range, so we'll be able to stay in contact.'

Rose looked at him and stepped back a little. 'Ah, if we need you, we'll find you,' she said.

Dru shrugged, and returned the walkie-talkie to his bag.

Jacob and Rose headed off, Rose helping Jacob with his sore leg.

Now Dru was unable to stop himself from yawning. He looked at his watch. 'Wow. I didn't realise we'd been gone for so long.'

'Vidya better have covered for us,' said Kal.

'Let's get home,' said Dru.

After a train trip and a bike ride, the boys arrived at their house just as the sun was rising. They quietly parked their bikes down the side of the house, snuck in the front door and tiptoed up the stairs to their bedroom.

Dru crawled into his bed fully clothed. 'Oh . . .

bed,' he moaned with happiness. Every inch of him craved sleep. His eyes drifted shut.

Kal pulled the curtains closed, climbed into his bed and fell asleep. It felt like they were only asleep for five minutes when Dru heard Dadi outside their bedroom door. 'Time to wake up, my little wombats!'

'No, no, no, no,' moaned Dru, eyes wide open.

'Come on, boys, don't insult my breakfast by letting it go cold!'

She opened the curtains, filling the room with morning light.

Dru groaned, burying his head under his pillow.

CHAPTER FOURTEEN

Morning sun streamed across the kitchen bench loaded with aloo parathas, raita and spicy mango achaar. Dru, mostly asleep, sat at the bench chewing his food slowly, as though eating Dadi's food was hard work.

Kal, on the other hand, looked like he'd managed a good night's sleep, and was ready to face the day with one hundred per cent energy. He hungrily loaded up his plate with more parathas.

Dadi brought out more food, dancing to Bollywood music on the radio. 'Who wants more parathas?'

'Me!' exclaimed Kal. 'I'm starving.'

'That's my boy,' responded Dadi. She looked over at her other grandson. 'Come on, Dru, keep up with your brother!'

Vidya eyed the twins angrily as Dadi moved towards the pantry. 'You two owe me,' she said under her breath. 'I totally covered for you last night. I had to do hours of kabaddi practice with Dadi. It was torture.'

Kal laughed.

Vidya glowered at him. 'Give me your phone.'

Kal handed his phone to Vidya. She flipped through the stored files until she found the offending video of her dancing in front of the mirror. She deleted it with a satisfied smirk. 'That better be the only copy.' She handed the phone back to Kal.

'It is.'

Anousha entered the kitchen, looking fresh, high ponytail, sweat pants, jersey and runners, ready for exercise. She kissed Dru's head, then removed a dead leaf from his hair. 'You need to shower, *chotu.*'

Anousha picked up a paratha, but before she could raise it to her mouth Rahul, dressed for work, came up behind her and cheekily took it, taking a big bite.

'Hey!' said Anousha.

Rahul, with his mouth full of paratha, said, 'You snooze, you lose.'

'Sit down, sit down,' said Dadi.

Rahul shook his head. 'Sorry, Mum, the bakery needs me.'

Anousha grabbed another paratha. 'And I'm on my way to the gym before the lab.'

Dadi was faux outraged. 'What kind of example is this? Neglecting family breakfast time?'

Rahul gave his mum a quick kiss and all was forgiven.

As his parents left the kitchen, Kal held up another phone and showed it to Vidya. It played the same video Vidya had just deleted.

'Oh, what's this on *Dru's* phone?' said Kal, baiting his sister.

Vidya was instantly furious. 'Delete it! Now!' she demanded. She jumped out of her chair to grab the phone but Kal was too quick for her. He also jumped up, and ran. Vidya chased Kal around the kitchen, as he sang along to Vidya on the video.

As Dadi scolded the siblings for being so raucous at breakfast time, Dru, alone at the bench, leaned his head on his hand. His eyes closed as complete mayhem continued around him.

•

'Dru!'

Dru was sleeping in a bed made of doughnuts, sweet-smelling and ever so soft.

'Drupad Sharma!'

Dru's eyes snapped open. There were no doughnuts. Only an angry teacher and a class full of students laughing at him.

'Are we keeping you up?' Mr Park asked sarcastically.

'Uh, no, Mr Park.'

Regan sneered at Dru and he blushed.

'I mean, yes, I mean I'm awake,' said Dru, trying to salvage the situation.

'In that case, maybe you can tell us the answer

to the equation on the board?' suggested Mr Park, looking in confusion at this strange behaviour from his best student.

Dru looked at the complicated equation on the board but his brain was not quite up to speed. 'Um . . . if you multiply the –'

He didn't get a chance to continue because he was interrupted by a loud, sharp knock on the classroom door.

'One moment, class,' said Mr Park as he went over to talk to Miss Biggs.

Dru knew he should spend the extra time working out the answer to the maths problem but he was just so tired. He looked over to Kal, who seemed very alert, and was entertaining the kids around him by juggling pens.

'How come you're so awake?' asked Dru resentfully.

Kal flexed an arm muscle and continued to juggle.

Mr Park stepped back inside the classroom. 'Okay, like you guys I'm not overly thrilled with all the Global Child stuff happening around here, but today they have commandeered my class and looks like I've scored a free period. You, however, have not been so lucky. You can finish that equation for homework, making sure you show all the workings along the way. Now Miss Biggs will take over the rest of the lesson.'

Dru looked over at Miss Biggs and noticed a small orange badge on her lapel. Still feeling a little foggy from his doughnut dream, he knew there was a significance to the badge but he couldn't quite recall . . . someone had said . . . that was it! Rose had mentioned the orange badges.

As Mr Park left the classroom, Dru whispered to Kal. 'Kal! Miss Biggs. Look at what she's wearing.'

Kal looked from Miss Biggs back to Dru and just shrugged quizzically.

Miss Biggs smiled. 'I have some exciting news. This class will all be participating in the Global Child Initiative's leadership program. To kick it off, I am happy to announce your new Year Leader . . .'

Kal rolled his eyes at Dru and mumbled under his breath, 'Don't say Regan . . .'

'Regan Holcroft!' announced Miss Biggs.

Regan, delighted, jumped up from her seat, as Miss Biggs led the class in half-hearted applause.

'Thank you. Thank you, everybody,' said Regan, beaming.

'Thanks, Regan. Now everyone please follow me to the quadrangle, where we will participate in a wellness activity,' ordered Miss Biggs.

The students looked at each other, surprised. It was starting to feel as though they never spent any time in the classroom. And what exactly was a 'wellness activity', anyway?

•

Once the class arrived at the quadrangle, Miss Biggs clapped her hands. 'Form neat lines, please, everyone.'

Regan was upfront, trying to boss the kids around.

'Neat lines!' she parroted.

Reluctantly, the students fell in to line.

Miss Biggs turned to Regan. 'Regan, now that you are Year Leader, it's even more important that you report any suspicious activity to me.'

'I understand, Miss Biggs,' said Regan. 'I actually have something you should look at.'

Regan took out her phone and showed Miss Biggs a video of Kal kicking a rubbish bin against a brick wall, leaving it totally smashed. Miss Biggs looked at it, assessing. 'Interesting. When did this take place?'

'Yesterday,' said Regan. 'At Multicultural Day.'

'Kal Sharma did that to a metal bin with one kick? That's remarkable.'

This was not the response Regan was looking for. 'Do you mean he's not in trouble?' she asked, hoping she'd misunderstood the Wellness Officer's response.

Miss Biggs gave a thin smile. 'Thanks for bringing it to my attention, Regan. In line now, please.' Miss Biggs brought out her tablet and started to tap in numbers on the digital keyboard.

Disappointed, Regan joined the line, muttering to herself, 'Kal should get a detention. That bin is school property.'

Dru was next to Kal in the line. 'Did you see that Miss Biggs is wearing an orange badge?' he whispered.

There was no response from Kal and Dru looked around, noticing that all the students around him had stiffened. Their fingers twitched, and their eyes were wide open, staring straight ahead. Thinking fast, he mimicked them. He glanced at Miss Biggs, who was staring at her tablet, then Dru shifted behind a taller boy, Nathan, so as to be out of her direct eye line.

Without any instruction, the students began to move in unison – one step forwards, and then they all turned right, except for Dru, who was so stressed he turned left by accident before correcting himself. Luckily, Nathan was still helping him keep out of view of Miss Biggs and her tablet. They all turned left, and then stepped back into their original position. Dru followed a split-second behind, wondering how long this was going to go on for. He was uncoordinated at the best of times and this was not the best of times.

After a couple more movements, the students turned to face Miss Biggs, and a moment later the students relaxed back into their normal postures, the 'spell' broken.

Miss Biggs checked her wristwatch as the school bell rang. The kids were no longer controlled by anything or anyone, and started to chat and walk back to the school to gather their bags and head home.

Miss Biggs smiled after them. 'Enjoy your afternoon, children.'

'Is that it?' Kal asked Dru before giving a shrug. 'Not much of a wellness activity.' He jogged off to pick up his school bag, leaving Dru shell-shocked. He had really hoped the terrifying classroom test moment of days ago would never happen again. But whatever the experiment was, it was continuing.

•

As the boys rode home, Dru was finally able to tell Kal what he'd witnessed.

Kal was incredulous. 'You're saying we were marching around like zombies?'

'Do you really not remember any of it?' asked Dru, surprised.

Kal thought hard. 'I remember going to the

quadrangle. And I remember the bell ringing at the end of the day. In between it's just, like, whatever.'

'Whatever?' said Dru, not appreciating Kal's laidback response. 'Kal, they're controlling your minds and you're not even aware they're doing it!'

Kal shrugged. 'But I don't feel any different.'

'Miss Biggs had an orange badge on her jacket pocket. The Unlisted warned me about those.'

Kal looked blasé, so Dru helped him put two and two together. 'So, that means that Miss Biggs is most likely a senior member of Infinity Group.'

They were coming out of the tunnel under the train line when a hooded figure stepped out in front of their bikes. The twins, freaked, swerved and almost crashed.

The figure pulled back her hood.

Dru's heart was beating so loudly he was sure the whole neighbourhood could hear it. 'Rose?'

Rose looked frightened. 'We need your help. It's Jacob.'

CHAPTER FIFTEEN

Jacob lay on one of the cardboard beds, shivering and sweating. The tear in his capri pants exposed the cut on his leg, which was now swollen and red – clearly infected.

Kymara was freaking out. 'Is he gonna die? He's gonna die, isn't he?'

Gemma glared at Kymara, all the while pacing anxiously around their hide-out. 'I don't know, Kymara. Just . . . stop talking for two seconds.'

Jacob raised his head. 'Chill. I'm not going to die.' He lay on an old sleeping-bag they had found near a dumpster. Beads of sweat gathered across his forehead. He grimaced in pain.

All three teens heard a sudden noise from inside a nearby tunnel, and held their breath. A second later Rose appeared in the entrance.

'He's got worse, Rose! What are we going to do?'

'Dru's meeting me at the tunnel entrance in an hour,' said Rose, taking control. ' We can't buy medicine, but he can bring some.'

'Either that or a squad of Infinity Group guards,' said Kymara.

Rose and Gemma exchanged a worried look.

Kymara sighed, then tried to lighten the mood. 'I mean, I hope it's the medicine. Obviously.'

•

After letting Dadi know they'd be late home from school, Dru and Kal sat in the waiting room of the small neighbourhood doctor's surgery where their aunt worked. The boys had visited their aunt at work with Dadi, but had never visited the surgery alone before.

Both boys were fidgety and nervous. The receptionist looked over at them and Kal flashed her a charming smile. Dru couldn't do anything but grimace; he was feeling sick with nerves and exhaustion.

'Rose said he has a fever,' Dru said to his brother, 'which means Jacob's cut has probably got infected.'

'Yeah, sounds right,' said Kal. 'Remember that happened to me last year after I stood on the oyster shells at Little Bay?'

Dru nodded. 'Yeah, you needed antibiotics.'

Kal nodded. 'They tasted awful. The pills were really big.'

Dru tried to keep the conversation on track. 'So, I think we need to get antibiotics for Jacob.'

Kal agreed. 'Once we're in Bua's office, you create a distraction, and I'll look around for the medicine.'

Dru wasn't sure that was the right way to tackle the problem. 'I think we have to tell Bua what's happened. She's a doctor and Jacob may need more than just antibiotics.'

Maya walked out of her office with an elderly

patient, giving her a warm tap on the arm. 'Nancy, you let me know if it hasn't cleared up by next week. Okay, dear?'

Nancy nodded and headed for the reception desk. Dr Sharma was about to call her next patient when she noticed her nephews. 'Hello! What are you two doing here?'

Kal stood up. 'We just came to see our favourite bua!'

With a big smile, Kal ran over to Maya and hugged her tight.

'Your favourite and your *only* bua,' she remarked wryly. She looked towards the reception desk, and the receptionist said, 'Your next patient's running late. He won't be here until after five.'

Maya nodded. 'Okay boys, into my office.'

'So, how are things?' she said as they entered her office and she took a seat behind her desk. 'You look tired, Dru.'

'Uh . . . that's why we're here,' said Kal. 'Dru needs to talk to you about something personal.'

'What?' said Dru. They hadn't planned what the 'distraction' was going to be but this didn't sound promising.

Maya put on her soothing doctor voice. 'Don't be embarrassed, Dru. You're at the age now where things start changing. Your voice, your emotions, parts of your body . . .'

'It's that last one. I'll give you some privacy,' Kal offered, standing up and moving over to the side of the room that housed the medical supplies.

Maya stood up and moved closer to Dru, which meant she couldn't see what Kal was doing.

Kal signalled for Dru to keep talking.

Maya took Dru's hand. 'Where are you experiencing changes? Is it your –'

Dru interrupted before Maya could finish her question and say anything embarrassing. 'It's my feet!' he almost yelled.

Kal had managed to silently open a drawer, and was looking at packets of medicine.

Maya stared at Dru. 'Your *feet* are changing? How?'

Dru was panicking. 'Yep. My . . . toes are, like . . .' Dru looked up to see Kal about to knock over a holder filled with pencils. 'Pencils,' he said too loudly.

Kal caught the pencil holder before it tipped over.

Maya looked concerned. 'Toes like pencils? That sounds bad, Dru. Take your shoes off, and I'll get my –' Maya turned around to see Kal holding a packet of paracetamol.

'Kal, what are you doing?' she asked, surprised.

Kal tried to look casual. 'Looking for medicine. For Dru's pencil toes.'

Maya looked from one twin to the other, frowning. The soothing doctor voice had disappeared. 'Okay, you two. Tell me what's going on right this second.'

The twins said nothing. 'What's this pencil-toe rubbish anyway?' Maya walked over to the phone on her desk and picked up the receiver. 'I'm calling your father. Or worse, your dadi.'

Kal put up his hands. 'No! No!'

'We can explain,' said Dru.

'Dru,' warned Kal.

'We need antibiotics,' blurted out Dru.

Kal glared at him. 'What about sticking to the plan, bro?'

'I have to tell Bua,' he said to Kal.

Maya slowly put down the phone, watching them both carefully.

Dru turned to his aunt. 'A boy we know is sick. His leg got infected. It's bad.'

Maya nodded. 'That's serious. His parents should take him to hospital immediately. I don't keep medicine in my office. I write a prescription and then the patient picks up the medicine from the chemist. You know how it works, boys.'

Dru frowned, not sure how to describe the situation. 'We know, but we need you. Our friend needs you. He's – ah – on his own and can't be moved.'

Maya frowned. 'What do you mean, can't be moved?' she asked.

'Please, Bua. I can't explain everything, but you're the only one who can help,' pleaded Dru.

Maya looked over at Kal, who nodded in agreement. 'Please, Bua, we need you.'

Their aunt couldn't resist her nephews' request for long, and eventually she agreed to drive them to the city, where their 'friend' was.

Once the three of them arrived outside the tunnel entrance, Maya looked around. 'He's in a *tunnel*? I have to report this.'

She had her medical bag with her but looked like she wasn't willing to take this doctor's visit any further.

'I told you this would happen,' Kal sniped at Dru.

Dru wasn't ready to give up just yet. 'You're a doctor. That means you have to keep secrets and stuff, right? The Hippo's Oath.'

Maya tried not to smile as she corrected her nephew. 'The Hippocratic Oath, yes.'

Dru remained serious. 'This boy's in danger and you can't tell anyone where he is. You need to promise us.'

Maya sighed heavily. All three of them knew this was highly unorthodox, but it was also clear that the twins thought they were trying to do the right thing.

'I really don't want to do this, it's against the law, I could lose my licence,' she said reluctantly. Dru looked at her with pleading eyes. She sighed, 'Just take me to the child so I can treat him.'

Dru stepped forwards towards the gate at the tunnel entrance, and the other two followed.

Dru turned around and said to Kal, 'You can't come in, you need to wait up on the hill, away from here.'

Kal groaned. 'I hate this.' But his brother was right.

'Why can't he come in?' asked Maya.

Dru and Kal look at Maya, tight-lipped.

'Something else I'm not allowed to know,' she said. 'Right.'

Kal stayed put as Dru began squeezing through the gate and into the tunnel.

CHAPTER **SIXTEEN**

When Dru and Maya had walked into the tunnels a short distance, Dru stopped and warily called out, 'Hello? Rose?' Then he mimicked the whistle that Rose had given last night to find Jacob, and waited in the silence.

Maya had not dressed with tunnelling in mind, and was staring at the dirty water on the ground to her suede shoes when Rose and Gemma emerged from the darkness.

'Dru. Did you bring the medicine?' asked Rose.

'Yeah,' replied Dru. 'But there's something else you need to know.'

'What?' asked Gemma.

Maya stepped up, making herself known. 'My name is Dr Sharma.'

The girls were horrified. 'No!' exclaimed Gemma.

'What have you done?' asked Rose as both girls ran back into the tunnels.

Dru called out to them. 'Wait! You can trust her!'

Maya turned to Dru. 'What's happening, Dru?'

'They're scared. We have to talk to them. Come on.'

Dru and Maya walked deeper into the tunnels. 'Guys?' Dru called out. 'This is my aunty. She's a doctor.'

Suddenly, Dru's leg snagged on a trip-wire. A bunch of bottles that had been strung up on string fell from above. 'Ow!' Dru covered his head. 'Seriously?'

Maya was not impressed. 'Is this some sort of silly game?' she asked Dru.

Dru shook his head.

•

Further in the tunnel system, Gemma and Rose were crouched by Kymara. They looked at her quizzically.

Kymara shrugged. 'I had a bit of spare time.'

'Time to roll out,' said Gemma. The girls grabbed some large wooden spindles from a stockpile and started rolling them down the tunnel ahead of them.

•

At Dru's end, he was kicking away a plastic bottle and considering moving forwards as Maya peered into the darkness ahead of them. 'Do you hear something?' she asked, worried.

Suddenly wooden spindles came rolling at them, almost knocking them off their feet. They jumped out of the way.

Maya scoffed angrily. 'This is ridiculous.'

Dru was desperate. He shouted out to the girls. 'What are you doing?'

The girls yelled back as the spindles kept rolling. 'Just leave us alone!' said Gemma.

'You broke your promise!' shouted Rose.

'I had to!' responded Dru. 'My aunt's the only one who can save Jacob!'

Maya stepped forwards and called out. 'If your friend's wound is infected, he could develop sepsis. He could die without medical attention!'

Dru shouted: 'It's like you said, Rose, if we're going to survive, we need friends!'

The spindles stopped rolling. There was silence from the girls. After a moment, Rose walked through the tunnel towards them. 'Don't make me regret this,' she said to Dru as she led him and his aunt to the hide-out.

Maya looked around, her face showing grave concern as she entered the teens' makeshift living area. It was wet and dirty and no place for someone who was seriously hurt. She clocked Jacob lying on a flattened box. She rushed over and started to check his vital signs. 'Hi, I'm Maya. I'm here to look after you.'

Jacob lay still as Maya continued her medical check. 'Heartbeat and respiration are raised – and he's running a fever.' Maya pulled a small bottle of hand sanitiser out of her bag and threw it to Dru. 'Wash your hands with that, put these on.' She handed him a box of rubber gloves and turned to Rose, 'And you?'

'Rose.'

'You too. We can't run the risk of a secondary infection.' Maya gestured for Dru to move to Jacob. 'Lift his leg and keep it elevated,' she said. Maya removed bandages, antiseptic creams and medication from her bag.

'What's all that?' asked Gemma.

'Antibiotics and I'm giving something for the pain.' She prepared a needle, swabbed his arm and injected a painkiller in his arm. 'He should be in hospital on a drip, but this will have to do.'

Maya removed some cotton swabs from a packet, then handed them to Rose. 'I'll need you to pass these to me.'

Rose nodded as Maya moved to Jacob's leg. She said to Jacob gently, 'This is going to sting a little.'

Jacob winced in pain as she began to clean the wound, Rose assisting. Dru stood a little way back – the sight of blood left him woozy – and it didn't take long before Jacob was feeling better. He tried to sit up, but Maya discouraged movement.

'You need to rest.'

Rose looked at her friend. 'You better listen to her. She just saved your life.'

Jacob glanced down at the bandage on his calf. 'I'm starving. Did you bring food?' he asked with a croaky voice.

Everyone laughed, relieved Jacob was feeling well enough to be thinking of his stomach again.

•

Rose walked Dru and Maya back to the tunnel entrance but stayed hidden as they stepped outside.

'Is he all right?' asked Kal, who stood waiting with a shopping bag.

'He'll live,' said Maya. 'But he shouldn't stay in there – it's not sanitary. He needs to be in a hospital.'

Rose shook her head. 'No hospitals.'

Maya looked back at her curiously. 'Where are your parents? Who are you hiding from?'

'It's better you don't ask,' Dru answered for Rose.

Maya shook her head, annoyed at what she obviously saw as childish secrecy. 'Remember what I said: fresh bandages every twelve hours, keep up the medication, and plenty of fluids.'

Rose nodded solemnly. 'We will. Thanks.'

'And call me if he gets worse,' finished Maya.

Dru handed Rose one of the walkie-talkies. 'You have to take this. It's the only way you can be sure of safely reaching us from this distance. And it'll save you from running round the streets looking for us.'

Rose watched him for a moment then nodded and accepted Dru's gift. They exchanged weary smiles.

Kal took a Western Sydney Wanderers scarf out of the shopping bag, and handed the scarf to Rose. 'Could you give this to Jacob?' said Kal.

She unfurled the scarf, curious.

'Tell him Kal said, "Go Wanderers".'

Rose smiled. Kal handed her the bag filled with food and drink, which Rose took gratefully before she headed back into the gloomy darkness of the tunnel system.

•

Maya drove Kal and Dru back to the surgery, where they'd left their bikes. All three were tired and strained.

They got out of the car and Maya looked at her nephews. 'I should report this to Child Services.'

Dru frowned. 'But you won't. Right?'

'How do you even know these kids?' asked Maya.

The twins looked at each other, remaining silent.

'You're putting me in an impossible position. This isn't a game,' said Maya, frustrated. 'It's life and death.'

'We know that,' said Kal.

'I don't think you do,' she said. She sighed. 'Now get home before your dadi kills all three of us.'

'Thank you, Bua,' said Dru.

'Yeah, thanks,' added Kal.

The boys trudged back to the side of the surgery, over to their bikes. 'You should have let me take care of things today,' said Kal. 'Your new friends have put Bua in danger.'

Dru wasn't focused on what Kal was saying. Instead,

he was watching their aunt. Kal followed his brother's gaze.

She had crossed the road outside the train station, and was talking to a man and a woman who were standing next to a Global Child Initiative car. She shook hands with them warmly and then got into the back seat of their car. The man and woman, wearing suits with orange badges pinned to their lapels, scanned the surrounding area.

The boys shifted around the corner out of sight, but kept watch.

The man and woman got into the car and drove away, with Maya Sharma inside.

Dru turned to his brother, the combination of fear and exhaustion hitting him hard. 'You think the Unlisted have put Bua in danger?' he asked. 'What if it's the other way around?'

Kal shook his head, unsure about what he'd just seen. Had Dru just revealed the whereabouts of Rose and the other tunnel kids to the sinister Global Child Initiative? Did they now have to fear their families as well?

CHAPTER SEVENTEEN

Early the next morning, Sydney city was just beginning to wake up. Kookaburras squawked, the ibis in Hyde Park went looking for leftover rubbish scraps as council trucks drove around emptying the bins. Near the tunnel entrance, a large white truck squealed to a stop. Men jumped down out of the truck and started to unpack heavy equipment, hauling it towards the tunnel entrance.

Inside the tunnel system, Kymara, Gemma and Jacob were sleeping in old sleeping-bags and dirty blankets, curled up. Gemma was in the midst of a dream, tossing and turning.

But Rose, a small distance away from the others, lay awake, completely still, eyes open, listening. Something didn't feel right but she couldn't tell what it was and didn't want to wake the others if she was being paranoid.

She decided she was imagining things and started to shut her eyes again when the sound of a metal pipe dropping further up the tunnel system made her jump to her feet, super alert. She pulled on her shoes and whisper-shouted to the others, 'Hey, wake up! We have to go!' She grabbed a nearby backpack and started throwing in anything of use: leftover food, clothes and their bedding.

Gemma and Jacob were still shaking off sleep, but they did as they were told. They rolled up their blankets, and put their shoes on as quickly as they could.

Kymara was not a morning person, and she was much slower to respond.

Rose moved over to her. 'Move!'

Kymara rolled her eyes. 'Is this one of your stupid drills, Rose? I'm so not in the –'

The end of her sentence was cut off by the sound of a loud *clang*. A heavy piece of metal fell to the ground, its echo bouncing along the walls of the tunnels.

Kymara was no longer sluggish. She jumped up, gathered her belongings.

'Turn off the alarm system,' said Rose. 'We don't want anyone to know we've been here.'

Kymara nodded, grabbed the alarm equipment, undid the wiring and stuffed it into her backpack.

Rose quickly scanned the area, shuffling some newspaper and toppling the milk crates to make it look like no-one had been staying there. She looked to Gemma, Kymara and Jacob, and pointed further down the tunnels, away from the direction the noise had come from. 'Run!' she said. The three didn't need to be told twice. They raced off, Rose bringing up the rear.

Back at the entrance of the tunnels, men in orange jumpsuits entered the tunnels, wearing goggles and gas masks. They stomped through the muck, torches lighting the way. No-one spoke as they moved further into the darkness.

•

At the Sharma household, all was quiet. Kal was sleeping deeply, but Dru, already awake and dressed in his school uniform, was whispering into the walkie-talkie. 'Rose . . . Rose . . . can you hear me?'

Frustrated by the lack of response, he moved over to his brother's bed and tried to shake him awake. 'Kal!'

Kal opened one eye and stared up at his twin. 'Watching me sleep is creepy, bro.'

'You sleep like the dead,' said Dru.

Kal squinted at his digital watch. 'It's five-thirty in the morning. Why are you waking me at five-thirty in the morning?' Kal started to roll over, ready to fall back asleep.

'I know it's early, but I can't get hold of Rose. I tried calling them last night when we got back but there was no response. And this morning she is still not answering.'

'Maybe she's trying to sleep too?' suggested Kal gruffly.

'If Bua told Infinity Group about Rose and the

others, they might be in real trouble,' explained Dru. 'We have to check on them.'

Kal, tired, brushed Dru off. 'You go.'

Dru wasn't impressed. 'It's safer if we don't split up, remember?'

'I know,' said Kal, stifling a yawn, 'but one of us needs to stay here and cover.'

Dru grabbed his backpack and headed out the door. 'All right. See you at school.'

Kal fluffed his pillow, adjusted his doona and lay down, willing himself to fall back asleep, but he lay still instead, with his eyes open, looking up at the ceiling.

After an hour and a half of not sleeping, he went downstairs to find Dadi in the kitchen, organising breakfast. The table was already covered with deliciousness – the smell of samosas and *kachoris* made Kal's mouth water. Kal glanced at the calendar on the fridge and noticed that in big glittery letters under today's date were the words DADI'S BIRTHDAY.

Vidya entered the kitchen and spied the spread

appreciatively. 'Morning, Dadi. Loving the special fry-up.' She moved towards the kitchen bench.

Kal, already feeling smug, gave Dadi a kiss and a hug. 'Happy birthday, Dadi!'

Vidya's eyes widened. *Oops!*

Dadi gave Kal an extra-warm hug in return. 'Thank you, my favourite grandchild.'

Kal sat down at the kitchen bench and began to tuck in.

Vidya rushed back to her grandmother. 'Happy birthday, Dadi. I didn't forget, I just . . .' She wasn't sure of her excuse.

'You were too excited by the feast you saw in front of you?' she offered with a generous twinkle in her eye.

'Exactly,' said Vidya, relieved.

Dadi ruffled Vidya's hair affectionately. 'Is Dru on his way?' she asked Kal.

Kal had his mouth full of kachori and attempted to speak.

Dadi stopped him. 'Ah, don't talk. Chew or you'll choke.'

Anousha and Rahul arrived in the kitchen. Anousha was already in work clothes, handbag on shoulder. She looked ready to speed out the door but stopped to give Dadi a kiss. 'Happy birthday,' she said.

Rahul followed with a hug and a kiss.

Dadi was never happier than when her family was around her, eating her cooking. She served her son a samosa and he added a delicious homemade coriander chutney.

'Where's Dru?' asked Anousha.

'He wanted to go to the library before school for . . . something,' answered Kal, not making eye contact with anyone. He knew from experience he wasn't great at lying.

Rahul was mock-proud. 'He gets it from me. So industrious, yah!' he said with a grin.

Anousha rolled her eyes. She was focused on Kal. 'Did you finish your maths homework?'

Kal remained noncommittal. 'Ye-ah, I think so.'

'I don't want to have to come in and talk with your maths teacher again,' warned Anousha.

'Don't worry, I don't want you to either,' answered Kal cheekily.

Anousha shot him a stern look.

'I did it. I promise,' said Kal, reaching over the table for more food, making his dadi smile.

Vidya, sitting next to him, said to her mum, 'Don't think he'd pass a lie detector . . . just sayin'.'

Kal whacked her on the arm. Vidya threatened to whack him back.

Dadi intervened. 'No fighting on my birthday.' As everyone finished up and started to leave for the day, Dadi sang out, 'Now remember, everyone back at six-thirty tonight for dinner. And then we will celebrate my *janam din* with no rushing around. Properly. No excuses.'

'Yes, Dadi,' the Sharma family replied in unison.

CHAPTER EIGHTEEN

Just as it was getting light Dru arrived near the tunnels, parking his bike a short distance away. He walked towards the tunnel entrance, looking around nervously, keeping an eye out for anything or anyone that might be an Infinity Group guard. He stopped breathing when he spotted a big white truck parked close by.

Outside the entrance to the tunnels temporary metal fencing had been put up, with a sign – 'DANGER – Keep Out. Authorised Personnel Only'. Dru wanted to run away right there and then, but knew he couldn't.

If it wasn't already too late, he wanted to warn Rose and the others.

Dru edged nearer the entrance. He noticed a few workers near the truck, stepping into hazmat suits. Gas canister-type equipment rested against a fence nearby.

He leaned down to tie his shoelace, surreptitiously taking in the action, trying to figure out a way to get inside the tunnels before the guys with the gas canisters entered.

Trying not to attract anyone's attention, he neared the entrance, and when he was sure no-one was looking in his direction, he wandered casually up to the fencing, and tried to move the heavy plastic foot quickly so he could slip in.

Unfortunately, it was so solid he could hardly shift it an inch. Luckily none of the workers were paying attention to the entrance, so after a bit of limbering up – arm stretches and a neck roll – he tried again. This time the concrete foot moved a teensy bit, just enough for him to shimmy through. Which was fortunate, because a couple of the workers started to wander over to the tunnel entrance. Dru darted inside, unseen. 'Here we go again,' he said as he entered the darkness.

He walked warily forwards in the half-light, feet splashing in dirty water. He couldn't remember the right way to the kids' hide-out, and he reached a place where he had to make a choice. There was a tunnel on the left and the tunnel on the right. They both looked identical. He stood there, undecided, when he heard a whistle that might have come from the tunnel on the left. Dru peered into the dark, and could just make out a shadowy figure but couldn't be certain if it was friend or foe.

From the tunnel on the right came a sudden flash of torchlight, blinding Dru.

A man's voice called out, 'Who's there?'

It definitely wasn't one of the Unlisted! And Dru wasn't going to stick around and find out exactly who it was. He turned and sprinted back to the entrance.

Behind him he heard heavy boots hitting the ground.

In his panic to get away, Dru tripped, landed in

a puddle, scrambled to his feet and raced towards the light. At the entrance, two men in bright orange hazmat suits were moving the temporary fence aside so they could enter the tunnel.

Dru tumbled out into the morning sunlight, surprising the two men.

'Where did you come from?' asked one of the men, confused by the sight of a frantic teenager fleeing the tunnel.

Dru wasn't going to hang around to answer. He sprinted away, dirty, confused and terrified.

•

Further inside the tunnel system, Rose sprinted back to Gemma, Kymara and Jacob, who were hiding in an alcove. 'I thought I saw Dru, but someone chased after him,' she said, breathing hard. 'And I think they're hauling in gas canisters.'

Gemma grabbed one of the old blankets and ripped strips from it. She frowned. 'Then we better wear masks,' she said, passing the strips to the others.

Rose nodded. 'Good idea.'

The four tied the makeshift masks over their mouths and noses, and at the sound of heavy footfalls heading closer towards them, the Unlisted started running further into the depths of the tunnels.

•

After his enormous breakfast, Kal biked to school, hoping Dru would already be there. Dru's bike wasn't at the bike rack, but the morning bell hadn't rung yet, so there was still time before his twin was missed.

Chloe wandered over to Kal, looking ill at ease. 'Hi. Where's Dru?'

'Dunno,' replied Kal.

'You normally ride to school together,' said Chloe.

'Not always,' countered Kal, wondering what Chloe was getting at.

'So, is he off sick today?' she continued.

Kal remained vague. 'He's around. Probably in the library,' he said, hoping Chloe wouldn't notice the absence of Dru's bike.

'Try the library,' Chloe shouted over to Regan, who was leaning against a wall, staring pointedly at Kal and Chloe.

Kal looked hard at Chloe. 'What're you doing?'

'She's Year Leader now, remember?' said Chloe.

'So?' answered Kal.

Chloe shrugged. 'She says I have to do what she says or she'll report me.'

Kal shook his head at Chloe's lame response.

'Bossy cow,' said Chloe, trying to sound lighthearted but her facial expression suggested otherwise.

Kal glanced back towards the school gate, willing his brother to appear before the bell rang, but there was no sign of him.

Once Kal got to the classroom, he watched as other kids trickled in. Regan was already in her favourite seat. 'Your brother wasn't in the library,' she said, with a smirk.

Kal was seriously worried, both about what Regan knew and about his brother's whereabouts. He was tossing up whether to find a way to be excused from class so he could go and search for his twin when Dru finally appeared at the classroom room, sweaty, dirty and with a serious case of helmet hair.

'What happened?' asked Kal as Dru sat down.

'I was too late. They –'

'Everyone get into class now, please,' the teacher said, before Dru could finish. 'Take a seat next to your study partner.' The boys exchanged concerned looks but didn't get a chance to talk further. Kal looked at his brother. 'What, they what?'

Dru could barely bring himself to look up. He swallowed hard.

CHAPTER NINETEEN

'Right, class,' said Mr Park, 'today we are going to . . .' he finished vaguely as the classroom door swung open and Miss Biggs appeared. 'Miss Biggs?' said Mr Park, rolling his eyes. He looked even more annoyed when she ushered in two people behind her – a man and a woman both wearing suits with orange badges highly visible on their lapels.

'Ah, you've multiplied, and these are?' asked Mr Park.

Miss Biggs scowled, ignoring the comment. 'Thanks, Mr Park, assessors from the Global Child

Initiative,' she said before leaving.

The two newcomers nodded at Mr Park, before scanning the class, moving to the back and taking a seat. The students were looking around at each other, creeped out. There was no explanation as to why they were there, and even Mr Park looked flustered by their presence in the classroom.

The man and woman, each wearing a black earpiece, took out electronic tablets and stared at their screens.

The class remained eerily quiet. No-one moved or spoke.

Mr Park smiled thinly. 'Ah, where was I?' He shuffled some papers on his desk. 'Yes, please pass your maths homework to the student next to you. We'll mark it as we go through the answers together.'

The students, grateful to break the uncomfortable silence, grabbed their homework books from their bags. Dru handed his book to the student next to him and received hers in return.

Kal looked around a little sheepishly, and didn't bother to take out his book.

'Okay, question one,' said the teacher. 'The volume of the cone is one third of the volume of the cylinder –'

The classroom door opened once again, and this time it was Dru and Kal who looked on in shock as Tim Hale walked in.

'Tim. Nice of you to join us,' said Mr Park sarcastically. 'You're late.'

'Tim, over here!' Kal called out, gesturing to the spare seat next to him.

Tim walked towards Kal, but as Kal went to high-five him the woman at the back of the class cleared her throat and he changed tack. Tim ignored his friend, walking straight past him and sat down near the adults at the back of class. He looked different, his curly hair looked more tamed and he had a blank stare on his face.

Mr Park sighed. 'Hopefully that's the last interruption for this morning. So, class, what is the volume of the cone?'

Regan's hand shot up.

'Yes, Regan?' asked Mr Park.

'Thirty-six,' she replied.

Kal turned back to Tim, puzzled by the ghosting, but Tim simply looked at Kal, expressionless, and then stared straight ahead again.

•

The morning class continued as normal, and it wasn't until recess that Dru got a chance to talk properly to his brother.

He found him on his way over to Tim, who was kicking a ball by himself.

'Kal?'

Kal frowned at his brother. 'Hang on, I need to find out where Tim's been.'

'But I have to tell you what happened this morning,' said Dru.

Kal was torn, but allowed Dru to pull him to the edge of the soccer field, where they were alone. 'What?' he asked.

'Rose and the others are in trouble,' blurted out Dru. 'The place was crawling with people in hazmat suits. Bua must have tipped off Infinity Group!'

Kal raised an eyebrow. 'I can't believe she'd do that.'

Dru wasn't sure either, but he *was* sure it wasn't a coincidence. He felt the anxiety of the past few days building. 'Maybe I was wrong. Maybe we should tell Mum and Dad what's going on.'

Kal disagreed. 'You saw what happened to Tim's parents.'

'But Tim's back,' said Dru, gesturing towards the boy who was still dribbling the soccer ball by himself. 'Maybe his parents are back too?'

'I'm going to talk to him,' said Kal as he jogged off towards his friend. 'Hey Tim!' he called out.

Tim turned to look at Kal, blank-faced. Dru watched as Kal ran up to Tim, chatting animatedly, while Tim seemed vague and disinterested.

The rest of the school day passed without incident. There were no fitness tests, no sick bay check-ups and no weird lapses into zombie-like behaviour from the class. But the two adults who had interrupted their morning maths class stayed for the rest of the day.

They didn't say anything or interact with the class, and if Dru concentrated hard enough on his work, he could almost forget they were in the class. But he couldn't help but steal looks at their orange badges.

After school, Dru and Kal headed over to the bike racks. On the way, they passed the female assessor talking to Regan. They couldn't hear what was being said but Regan looked like she was enjoying the attention. Dru looked worried. 'Did Tim tell you anything at recess?'

'I couldn't get an answer out of him on anything,' said Kal. 'It's like he wasn't really there, you know what I mean?'

Dru knew, and was seriously worried. 'What have they done to him?' he asked.

The twins fell silent. It was not a question either of them actually wanted an answer to.

'Did you get hold of the Unlisted?' asked Kal.

Dru had brought the walkie-talkie to school and had it tucked safely in his backpack. 'Still no answer.

Maybe we can find out more from Bua. Let's go to the surgery.'

Kal shook his head. 'You go. I've got soccer practice.'

'We can't keep splitting up,' said Dru. 'You said that Regan almost busted us this morning.'

'Don't you think people will notice if I'm not at training? We're meant to behave like normal, right?'

Dru eventually nodded, then put on his helmet and unlocked his bike.

Kal grabbed his sports kit from his backpack. 'We can talk to Bua at Dadi's birthday dinner tonight.'

'Dadi's birthday?!' said Dru.

Kal smirked. 'Yeah, she noticed you weren't there this morning.'

Dru was thinking ahead. 'We need to find out what's going on now. We might not have the chance with all the family around tonight. I'll go alone. Keep your head down and I'll see you at home.'

Kal nodded, and was about to jog off when Dru grabbed him by the arm. 'Wait.'

Dru watched the male assessor walk through the staff carpark and climb into a car boasting the GLOBAL CHILD INITIATIVE branding. The car drove out of the carpark and away.

Dru looked at his brother. 'Be careful.'

Kal nodded and jogged over to the soccer field. Dru looked both ways nervously, then cycled off in the opposite direction.

CHAPTER TWENTY

On the soccer field, Kal was happily warming up with the rest of the team. They were in two lines, one player holding the other's feet as they did sit-ups. After ten reps, they swapped. Regan was holding onto Kal's feet as he did sit-ups twice as fast as everyone else.

Regan was fuming. 'Stop showing off.'

Kal ignored her and sped up. He finished his set and Regan started hers. 'Where's your buddy Tim?' she asked.

Kal looked around. 'Why? Are you going to report him, Regan?'

Regan concentrated on her sit-ups, pleased she'd got a rise out of Kal.

The coach was walking down the line, doing a headcount. 'Where's Tim Hale? He can't miss another session or he's off the team.'

Kal jumped to his feet, eager to get away from Regan. 'I'll get him, coach. He must've forgotten. He lives just round the corner.'

The coach nodded. 'Don't be long.'

Kal sprinted off across the field, super-fast. The coach looked after him, impressed. 'Kal's fitness is through the roof.'

Regan looked after Kal, jealousy written all over her face.

•

As Dru approached Maya's surgery, everything seemed normal but he was reluctant to enter, unsure of what he would find. He stepped into the reception area and immediately his eyes were drawn to a new poster on the wall advertising the Global Child Initiative.

Beneath a photo of a school-aged child with her arms stretched towards a beautiful golden sunrise were the words: *Our Children. The World's Future.*

He gulped, suddenly feeling unwell. An elderly patient noticed Dru's fearful expression. 'Don't worry, son, you'll feel better soon.' She gave him a reassuring pat on the arm.

Dru tried to smile. 'Thanks. I hope so.' He walked over to the receptionist and she looked up at Dru. 'You were in yesterday, weren't you? Dr Sharma's nephew?'

'Yes. I was hoping I could see her again.'

The receptionist gave a sympathetic smile. 'She's not here today. She called in sick.'

The phone rang. The receptionist sighed, then answered the call.

Dru wasn't sure what to do. His bua prided herself on her good health and rarely suffered from illness, considering she spent so much time with sick people. And now she hadn't turned up for work the day after he'd seen her talking to those two people in the Global Child Initiative car? More than suspicious.

Dru's eyes were drawn back to the poster on his way out of the surgery. *Our Children. The World's Future.* He looked around, paranoid that someone was watching him. In just a few days Dru's future had changed, that was for sure, and it didn't seem nearly as hopeful as that girl on the poster was suggesting.

He was frustrated by all he didn't know. Had Rose, Jacob, Kymara and Gemma been rounded up by Infinity Group and . . . what? Would they have their personalities erased like Tim? Or worse?

To stop himself from having a full-scale panic attack, Dru made a decision. He was going to tell his parents about the craziness of the last few days. He had no choice.

•

Kal ran up to Tim Hale's front door and knocked on it, but there was no answer. He moved carefully around the side of the house to Tim's living-room window. He could see Tim sitting at the dining table, doing his homework. Kal tapped on the window.

Tim looked up, surprised, and opened the window. 'Hi Kal,' he said.

'We've got soccer practice, Tim. Remember?'

Tim looked vacant. 'Now?'

'Ten minutes ago,' said Kal. 'Coach says you have to come now or you're off the team.'

Tim glanced around the living room, then turned back to Kal and spoke to him like he was reciting lines. 'I have extra tutoring. Mum and Dad organised it before their business trip.'

Kal knew none of this was true, but he wasn't sure what he could do to get his friend to soccer practice. While he was weighing up his options, Tim looked back out of the living room again, nodded and left.

'Tim!' called out Kal.

The window remained open but Tim didn't return. 'Hello?' Kal called again. 'Who's there? Mrs Hale?'

Suddenly someone appeared at the window. It took a moment for Kal to register that it was the female assessor from the classroom. She stared at Kal, looked down at a tablet in her hand and then back at Kal. 'Are you Kal or Dru? Where's your twin? Is he nearby?'

She peered out the window, trying to catch sight of the twin she assumed was there because the device told her he was. Kal realised it was time to go. 'Ah, gotta go. Coming, Dru!' he yelled before sprinting away from Tim's house, leaving the assessor staring after him, frowning.

•

Dru arrived home and walked into the kitchen. Dadi was busy preparing dinner, watching one of her favourite old Bollywood films as she chopped vegetables. He was glad to see her after such a terrible day.

'Wombat!' she said, grabbing his face and giving him a big kiss. 'I missed you at breakfast this morning. It's not like you to miss my special day.'

'I'm so sorry. Happy birthday, Dadi.' He hugged her tightly.

Dadi looked closely at him. 'You look pale. Are you hungry?'

Dru shook his head. 'Is Kal home?'

'Still at soccer training,' said Dadi. 'But your dad's out the back. While I'm here cooking my own birthday dinner! Who would believe it? And no word from your bua.'

The mention of Maya brought back all of Dru's anxiety. 'I have to speak to Dad.' Dru was about to head outside when Kal flew into the room, rushing straight at his brother, almost tackling him to the floor. 'Dru. Wait!'

After grabbing some afternoon tea and making small talk, the twins went up to their bedroom and shut the door so they could speak in private. Kal sat on his bed, cross-legged, and explained what had happened at Tim's house. 'It was super creepy. There was no sign of his parents. And I think . . .' He trailed off, looking sheepish.

'What?' said Dru anxiously.

'She asked me if you were nearby,' said Kal.

Dru had not thought the day could get worse, but it just had. 'What? No!'

Kal nodded. 'She was looking at her tablet, and I think it must have been tracking my implants, so she assumed you were there too.' He looked guilty.

Dru was furious and scared. 'We never should have separated. Now nowhere's safe if we're not together.'

'Calm down, Dru,' said Kal. 'Otherwise Dadi will burst in with the fire extinguisher again.'

Despite the situation, Dru couldn't help but laugh at the memory. 'That *was* kind of funny.'

At the same time they both did their best Dadi impersonation: *'I don't like my wombats fighting!'*

After the laughing subsided, Dru sighed.

'Do you still want to tell Mum and Dad what's going on?' asked Kal cautiously.

'If Tim's parents are still missing . . .' He shook his head. 'Too risky.'

For what felt like the first time all day, the twins were in agreement, and it came as a relief to both boys. Before they could discuss the matter further, all of a sudden the unmistakable crackle of the walkie-talkie could be heard.

CHAPTER TWENTY-ONE

Dru and Kal agreed that if the tunnel kids were trying to get in touch with them via the walkie-talkies, there was a chance they needed the twins' help. The boys decided, without needing to speak to one another, that they would bike to the tunnels that afternoon. When they arrived at the entrance it was close to five o'clock and the worksite was deserted. But the metal pipes and wire fencing across the entrance remained in place.

'This is really heavy,' said Dru, pointing to the fence.

Kal yanked it with one hand and the fence moved

like the concrete foot was made of cardboard. Kal gave his twin a satisfied smile. 'Light as a feather.'

Dru rolled his eyes but they both knew he was grateful for his brother's strength right now.

Kal looked around. 'There's no sign of anyone here. I'm coming with you.'

'But the tracking?' said Dru.

'We don't know what's down there. You need me. And splitting up hasn't been working so well.'

Dru couldn't dispute Kal's logic. From his backpack he handed Kal a torch, pulled out another for himself and they tentatively entered the tunnels. 'Ready?' he said.

Dru strode ahead with his torch lighting the way.

Kal stepped in after his brother, flicking his torchlight around. 'Wow. Super cool. Who knew these tunnels even existed?' His torchlight shone on a large number of dead cockroaches scattered across the ground. 'Except for those.'

Kal walked a little further into the tunnel when suddenly his eyes glowed white and his fingers twitched.

He grabbed at the tunnel wall, dizzy, as though an electric shock had gone through him.

From further inside the tunnel, Dru looked back to his brother, and saw him grab hold of the wall. 'Kal, quit mucking around.'

When Kal fell to the ground and remained unmoving, Dru realised something was seriously wrong.

'Kal!' he shouted, and ran back to his brother.

The echo of 'Kal, Kal, Kal' bounced off the tunnel walls.

Dru crouched over his twin, shaking him. 'Talk to me, Kal. Are you okay?'

Kal was conscious, but dopey. 'Wh-what happened?'

Suddenly a hand clasped Dru's shoulder. Panicking, Dru swung his torchlight into the face of . . . Rose, who put her hands up to block the light. 'Hey,' she said, indicating the torchlight. 'Not in the eyes.'

Dru moved the beam away and saw that Jacob, Kymara and Gemma were right behind Rose. Kal sat up.

Relief flooded through Dru. 'You're okay?' he said to Rose. Without thinking he pulled her into a hug, then disentangled himself as awkwardness took over.

'They were council workers doing pest control,' explained Rose.

'We were only in danger if we had six legs,' said Kymara.

Rose looked over to Kal. 'What happened to you?'

'Nothing, just tripped,' he said nonchalantly, but he was a little shaky as he got to his feet.

Dru looked at Kal, confused about his lie, but he said nothing.

Gemma had moved over to the wall a little distance away. There were wooden panels partially hiding a vent they hadn't seen before. She bent down to it. 'Fresh air!' She moved the wooden panels away and tried to yank the metal vent free, but it wouldn't budge.

'Kal?' offered up Dru, pushing Kal forwards.

Kal tried to rip the metal vent loose, but couldn't. He and Dru both stood back in confusion. What had happened to his strength?

Jacob came to the rescue and pulled off the panel, being careful to place as little weight as possible on his injured leg. 'You're welcome,' he said cheekily, patting Kal on the back.

A tunnel shaft was revealed, big enough for the kids to climb into, just. Gemma wanted to investigate and immediately clambered in.

Kymara was less certain of climbing into dark shafts. 'Really?' she asked the others.

Rose shrugged, happy to head in after Gemma.

Jacob peered into the shaft. 'This better not be a sewage pipe.' He climbed in carefully after Rose.

Dru and Kal watched Kymara trying to make up her mind. 'I'm coming,' she finally called to the others as she hoisted herself up into the darkness.

The twins were left alone. 'Are you okay?'

Kal ignored his brother's concern. 'Bua wasn't trying to round up these guys, then. It was just pest control.'

Dru was unsure. 'We still have no explanation for why she was talking to Infinity Group guards last night. I still don't know if we can trust her,' he said.

Kal shrugged. 'You going in?' he asked, pointing to the shaft.

Dru climbed in and Kal, still feeling unwell but not wanting anyone to know, climbed in after him. The others were still moving slowly through the shaft.

'This is killing my knees,' complained Kymara.

'No-one fart,' said Jacob.

'So not funny, Jacob,' said Rose, pleased no-one could see the smile on her face.

Kal was struggling with the small space and still feeling terrible. 'How much longer?' he asked.

The shaft continued for a hundred metres more before opening out into a narrow staircase.

Climbing up a narrow set of steep stairs, Gemma moved further along another concrete tunnel until, all of a sudden, the space opened out into a large chamber with high ceilings. It was immediately obvious it had once been home to someone living rough. There was a battered, rat-chewed sofa leaning against a wall; old chip packets and newspapers littered the floor, and a few empty bottles used as candle holders were scattered around.

Gemma headed straight for a wide window where sunlight shone into the space. She stood in front of it, basking in the light it provided. She felt better than she had for days. The other kids entered the room moments later, looking around appreciatively.

'Wow!' said Rose, impressed.

Jacob headed over to the sofa and plonked down. Dust billowed and a couple of loose springs pinged but he still grinned like he'd won the lottery.

'Okay. This was worth the effort,' said Kymara with a grin.

Kal tumbled out last, looking unwell. He leaned against the wall, quiet.

Kymara zeroed in on an old radio in the corner of the room. She picked it up and rusted batteries fell out. It was only a temporary setback because Dru grabbed a torch from his backpack, unscrewed the end and handed her the batteries.

'Awesome!' She set to wiping the rust out of the battery compartment.

Jacob stretched out his leg, looking content. 'Legendary find, Gemma.'

Kymara pulled the radio antenna up and got a faint signal. Faint fifties rockabilly music played, which was not anyone's first choice, but no-one complained. 'Party time!' said Kymara with a fist pump.

Jacob did some quality sofa-dancing while Gemma and Rose danced together, bouncing around the room and holding each other's hands, laughing. This place was a huge improvement on their last hiding spot and everyone knew it.

Kymara tried to turn the dial on the radio, but it wouldn't budge. 'Oh man, the dial's broken. I guess we're stuck with this station then.'

Dru checked his watch and turned to Kal. 'We have to get back,' he said. 'Dadi's birthday.'

'Next time bring chocolate bickies,' suggested Rose.

Gemma agreed wholeheartedly. 'Lots of chocolate bickies.'

Jacob had a more discerning palate. 'Or maybe a fattoush salad with fresh parsley and –' he stopped when he saw everyone looking at him like he was crazy. 'Sure. Bickies, then. Great.'

Dru wished they could stay but Dadi would be wondering where they were. The twins said their goodbyes and headed back through the labyrinth.

As the twins approached the entrance of the tunnels Kal, looking sweaty and drained, suddenly straightened up, his eyes glowed and his fingers once again twitched. A barely perceptible jolt of electricity passed through his body. He wasn't sure what was going on, but he felt much better than he had for the past half-hour. Whatever had happened in the tunnels had been temporary . . . he hoped.

CHAPTER TWENTY-TWO

The boys rushed into the house at six thirty-five to find Vidya on her way to the kitchen carrying a beautifully wrapped parcel. She looked disdainfully at the boys. 'You remembered to get a present for Dadi, right?'

Kal and Dru looked at each other, horror on their faces.

Vidya raised an eyebrow – BIG TROUBLE – and walked into the kitchen.

The boys were frozen to the spot, both clueless about what to do next, when Rahul saw them looking guilty in the hallway. 'You're late, boys. Where have you been? There's no time to change.' He took in their dirty clothing. 'Which is a shame.' Rahul shook his head, then handed them each a wrapped present. 'Don't worry about your sister, she forgot too.'

'Thanks Dad,' said the boys, relieved, about to race into the kitchen.

'No, no. Sign the card first,' he added sternly.

•

When the boys entered the dining room, Dadi looked like a colourful Indian queen, sitting at the end of the table, unwrapping a gift. She was dressed in a bright orange silk sari with her hair piled high on her head. Anousha stood next to her, helping her remove the wrapping from the gift.

Two big bunches of flowers decorated the room and the table was set for a feast of curries, masalas and condiments.

Dadi smiled at her grandsons indulgently. 'Boys.

Come and give your dadi a kiss.' She put the unwrapped present aside, eyeing up the gifts they were holding. Her eyes twinkled. 'Now, your turn.'

The boys handed over their gifts, giving their grandmother a kiss. 'Happy birthday Dadi.'

'Look who remembered her mother's birthday after all,' said Dadi to the twins, referring to the boys' aunt, who brought over a large bowl filled with rice to the table.

Maya scoffed. 'As if I'd forget, Mum!' Dru stared at his aunty, trying to behave normally.

She took a seat at the table, next to Dru. 'I was worried you two weren't going to turn up,' she said smiling at him.

The twins looked at each other, heartbeats quickening.

•

The birthday dinner was epic, with the Sharmas declaring the feast the most delicious birthday dinner ever. Dadi was in full agreement, surprising even herself with her culinary expertise.

After the main meal was finished, the family brought out the birthday cake. As was the tradition, Dadi handfed a sliver of cake to her son and daughter, then she took another sliver and ate it herself. 'Here's to me,' said Dadi, thoroughly enjoying herself. 'Still as *javaan* as ever!' Dadi bowed playfully as the rest of the family clapped.

Maya leaned in to talk to Dru. 'Have you checked on your friend today?' she asked.

'Yes. He's okay,' answered Dru, reluctant to give too much away.

But Maya wasn't finished with the interrogation. 'Is he taking the medication I gave him? Are they still in those tunnels?'

'Not sure,' Kal answered for his brother. 'They move around a bit.'

'You know it's not safe for them there,' warned Maya.

Kal and Dru weren't sure whether their aunt's statement was a threat or merely concern. Dru felt like he had been winded, like the ground beneath him and Kal wasn't solid anymore. If they couldn't trust their aunty, who could they trust?

Dadi spoke. 'I know it's my special day, but my *beti* has an announcement to make.'

Maya looked immediately uncomfortable. 'Mum, not now.'

'Yes, now.' Dadi would not take no for an answer.

Maya sighed. 'Well,' she said, looking around the room at her family. 'I've been offered a job. I wasn't looking, but the opportunity was too good to pass up.'

Dadi was beaming with pride. 'Spit it out.'

'I've accepted a Medical Officer position with the Global Child Initiative,' said Maya with a smile.

Kal inhaled his cake rather than swallowed it. He coughed violently, crumbs flying.

Vidya responded like a typical big sister – with repulsion. 'Ew, Kal. You're meant to swallow the cake, not spit it everywhere.'

Dadi turned to Dru. 'Help your brother.' Dru obligingly tapped his brother on the back, but Dadi found his technique lacking. 'Not like that. Like *this*.'

She went to Kal and whacked him hard. 'Look up. Look up,' she yelled at him.

Kal, through watery eyes and wheezes, whispered, 'Not helping.'

Rahul handed Kal a glass of water, and he took a sip.

'Congratulations, Bua,' said Vidya.

'That's great news, Maya,' added Anousha.

Rahul turned to Maya. 'Well done, sis.'

'Very proud,' said Dadi. 'All she needs now is a nice doctor husband.'

Rahul found this very funny and chuckled at his sister's discomfort.

'Oh Mum, don't start that again,' said Maya. This was not the first time a boyfriend for Maya had been discussed. Nor would it be the last.

'Go team Sharma!' said Anousha with a big grin.

Maya smiled her gratitude at her sister-in-law, and then leaned in to Dru and Kal and spoke to them quietly but firmly. 'The Global Child Initiative can help your friends. I need you to bring them to the offices, or I'll have to report them to Child Services.'

The boys nodded grimly, not making eye contact with their aunt. They ate the rest of their cake in silence, as though it was a chore they had to get through.

The Sharma twins weren't yet sure how they were going to refuse their aunt's request, but they knew they had to. There was no way they were going to rat on the Unlisted, and now, on top of everything else, the threat had entered their own home. The boys were scared. How long could they keep Dru's secret from the Global Child Initiative when a member of their own family was so closely involved?

THE *UNLISTED* ARE COMING . . .

Dru and Kal Sharma, with the help of the underground Unlisted, are in a race against time to uncover the Infinity Group's plans for the world's youth. But as people begin to disappear, the twins can't be sure who to trust . . .

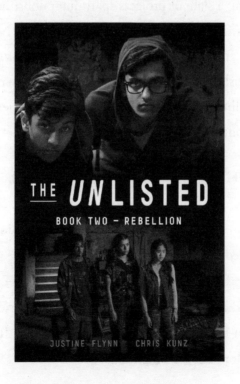

ABOUT THE AUTHORS

JUSTINE FLYNN has worked in film and television for 18 years in roles such as directing, producing, acquisitions, writing and development. Justine now works as an independent executive producer under her own company, Buster Productions, and is currently developing a slate of projects spanning publishing, TV and film, including *The Unlisted* for ABC/Netflix. Justine's first preschool book, *Miss Mae's Saturday*, was published in 2016. Currently, Justine is writing a feature film under the Create NSW Amplifier book adaptation initiative.

CHRIS KUNZ is a writer, editor and publisher who works across the TV, film and publishing industries. She has written and script edited for children's television, and has worked at various publishing houses, where she has been an editor and children's publisher. Chris created, storylined and wrote bestselling children's series with the Irwin family and Australia Zoo, and the RSPCA for Random House Australia.